The Adobe Castle

A Southwest Gothic Romance

Also by Inez Ross

The Strange Disappearance of Uncle Dudley:
A Child's Story of Los Alamos

and

The Bear and The Castle:
The James Oliver Curwood Story

The Adobe Castle

by Inez Ross

For Patti with best wishes

Inez Ross

Ashley House

Published by Ashley House
614 47th St
Los Alamos, New Mexico

Second Printing, 1999

ISBN: 0-9664337-3-4

Library of Congress Card Number: 98-93533

Printed in Canada

Since the eighteenth century, readers have been fascinated by any story which includes ghosts, a huge mysterious house, and an innocent newcomer caught in a web of dangerous intrigue.

Northanger Abbey by Jane Austen satirized the Gothic romances of that day. It was set in the English countryside and the resort town of Bath.

The Adobe Castle continues the tradition with the mountain setting of New Mexico near the popular resort town of Santa Fe.

The author wishes to thank Janice and Clive Caplan, Lois Whalen, and Lucille McCleskey for their encouragement and endorsements, and many friends for early editing and critiques: Leland, Lynette, Lois C., Jennifer, Miller T., Dotty, and the Los Alamos Writer's Group.

Thanks to Lane Warner for the suggested La Fonda menus, Connie Slocomb for the drawing of the Adobe Castle, S. Gunn and John Cole for digital layout.

Chapter I

Traveling is a fool's paradise.

—RALPH WALDO EMERSON

She would kill him right away, Heather decided. It was the best way to begin the entire scheme. She imagined the quick knife thrust, the agonized spastic reaction, the heavy slump of the body, the blood. Could she really stand a lot of blood? Any blood at all?

Her thoughts were interrupted by the conductor's call. "Lamy next! Lamy, New Mexico."

She had been waiting in the luggage bay corridor on the lower level of the Amtrak passenger coach behind a frazzled woman who was vainly trying to keep two children from climbing on the bags to see out the door. Already late, the Southwest Chief, enroute from Chicago to Los Angeles, had been delayed on a siding to let the eastbound

Chief pass before they could pull in to the little station stop.

The first-class passengers, now disembarking closer to the station, were dispersed by the time Heather and the other coach passengers walked the bumpy brick platform from the rear of the train. She felt unsteady to be on solid ground after almost twenty-four hours on the swaying coach, but the dry air, the dazzling sunshine, and the expectation of two weeks of freedom brought a surge of happiness and almost made her forget she didn't need to carry her bag. She stopped to unfold the handle and set the bag on its wheels, taking in the picturesque view of the little station with its curved Spanish arches and the big cottonwood trees.

Before she reached the station at the end of the bumpy brick walk, the big silver gray Chief had slid away toward Albuquerque and Los Angeles. The frazzled woman with her children was swept up by a crowd of relatives, and except for two boys who were looking for the pennies they had left to be flattened on the tracks, the platform was deserted.

Under the arched portico opposite the station was a large white van parked behind a sign that said SANTA FE SHUTTLE. The driver had climbed out and was headed toward her to take her bag. "Santa Fe?"

"No. Adobe Castle. I think I belong in this one." She nodded toward a brown van parked in the next slot. The label on the door said ADOBE VANS and its driver was engrossed on the pay phone at the corner of the building. She parked her bag in front of the van and waited. The driver seemed engaged in an exasperating conversation. As he talked on the phone he alternated gesturing into the air with his baseball cap and slapping it on his knee. "But she didn't come by train. I'm at the station now. I was here yesterday. Are you sure she didn't fly?"

Heather tapped him on the shoulder. "Are you looking for me?"

He turned around and smiled, his face displaying confused relief. "Talk to you later, Harry. I think the problem is solved." He hung up the phone and extended his hand. "Linda London? I'm Brian Minter."

"Heather McMarley. Are you the transportation to the Adobe Castle? I just got off the Chicago train."

"Sorry. No. I'm with Du Von Films. My passenger was supposed to arrive on the eastbound from Los Angeles. But if you're headed for Santa Fe, I'll be glad to take you."

"No thanks. I'd better wait for my own driver.

I have a reservation and am supposed to be met here."

"The Santa Fe shuttle has already gone. Taxis don't come out this far unless you call in advance. I'll wait while you call your hotel, in case you still need a ride."

He replaced his cap, smoothing back short wavy brown hair. Friendly blue eyes appraised her through small, round-lens glasses. He looked respectable enough: blue denim suit, white polo shirt, casual, yet professional. But there was something a little too friendly about the smile, she thought, and a little too self-assured about his suggestions. His smile had warmth, but his assurance implied an arrogant expression of power. He leaned against the van with arms crossed, confident that she would follow his directions.

"Thanks. But you don't need to wait. I'm sure he'll be here soon." She stepped to the phone and dialed the number on her reservation slip.

She was glad he could not hear the operator tell her, "I'm sorry. The number you have dialed is no longer in service. Please check the directory and try your call again."

"The line is busy," she told him. "I'll be fine. I don't want to delay you." She put on her best business demeanor and held up her head with what she assumed was a definite termination of the conversation. She knew where she had made her mistake. She had smiled first. Her practice teaching supervisor had told her that her trouble was her smile. Her long dark hair and ordinary features presented a pleasant and serious air. But her smile made her look far younger than her twenty-one years and took away the weight of her words, always weakening her credibility and undermining her authority.

He hesitated, and his aplomb seemed to vanish for an awkward moment. Then he conceded and, touching his cap in an old fashioned salute, gave her a quick "Good luck," climbed into the van and drove away.

She felt strangely disturbed. His Rhett Butler air had made her feel like Scarlett O'Hara, not the beautiful and determined heroine of the film, but the embarrassed young girl at the beginning of the novel. She recalled the opening of *Gone With the Wind* which related that Scarlett O'Hara was not beautiful. But she had charm. Heather felt that her own slim figure, dark hair, and fair Irish complexion may not be heroine quality, and she was not sure of her ability to charm, but she decided that her independent spirit could withstand the comparison favorably. She would not be ordered about, especially by a stranger.

There was no listing in the directory for any Adobe Castle. The information operator offered no help. Had she won a bogus prize at that drawing last year? But her travel agent had confirmed the reservation six months ago. She dropped the idea of calling the agent when she realized that the office, on Central Time, would be closed by now.

A call to the Santa Fe Taxi Shuttle was her last resort. A tired woman's voice answered with the recitation that regular runs outside the city had been discontinued for the day. But at the mention of Adobe Castle the dispatcher brightened and said, "Yes, I know where it is, and if you can wait till my shift ends, I can take you. It's an hour's drive into the mountains, but I live near there, so it'll be no problem. Go across the road to the Lamy Saloon and wait for me there. They have good sandwiches."

Following the dispatcher's suggestion, she found herself at a little bar table in the Saloon, which proved to be an upscale roadhouse catering to Santa Fe clientele with ample wallets. The pricey menu had an interesting history of the establishment printed on the back, and the waitress was willing to elaborate on the details.

"Ghosts? Yes, we have them. Never saw one myself, but we've come back in the morning to find the table settings all messed around after we set everything up and locked the doors the night before. Cook, he saw one once, standing behind the bar. He came back to the kitchen all white and looking about to faint. Told us to go look, but we didn't see it. Lots of old ranches around here are haunted. Adobe Castle, the resort hotel up the other side of Santa Fe, had a problem. The owner finally sold out. I guess there were other problems, but rumor had it that no one could sleep in the main wing and the power kept going out. I'm glad that our spirits here are the friendly kind. Can I get you some nachos?"

Heather's interest was piqued by the information and by the spicy snack. She wanted an adventure, and it seemed that she was about to have one. She remembered her promise to call home when she arrived and decided to call her grandfather while she was near a phone that worked. She would not tell him that she was not actually there yet. He had been difficult enough about letting her go, even threatening to send her brother Robbie along to make sure she was safe.

Since their parents had died in a car crash, Grampa McMarley had been mother, father, autocrat, and controller. For once Robbie was instrumental in persuading him that Heather should be allowed to go off by herself, to claim the prize she had won at the Suburban 10K, the yearly race that attracted enough runners and sponsors to offer lucrative prizes. She didn't win the race, but,eligible for the drawing by being a close finisher in her age division, had come home with a travel gift certificate for two weeks at this hotel in New Mexico.

The kind dispatcher was Betty Bergen, not as cheerful as she was chubby, with streaked blonde hair, Indian jewelry, and driving an old blue Ford sedan. Heather climbed in, eager to hear more about her destination, but Betty, whether from natural reticence or fatigue, at first declined to enter the easy familiarity that is usual in women's conversations, answering Heather's questions only briefly and reluctantly.

"You live near the Adobe Castle?"

"About two miles from there. My husband and I bought the Lazy-A Dude Ranch last year."

"That must be a job-and-a-half in itself. How many guests do you have?"

"Too many, in my estimation. We manage." The vague reply was given in a tone that seemed to end the conversation.

They rode in silence as their road straightened out, pointing toward the mountains. Skirting Santa Fe on a main highway, they turned off on a secondary road and began to climb. The sky darkened and the first raindrops came huge and heavy on the windshield, then gathered to become a deluge, complete with thunder and lightning. Betty, unfazed by the lowered visibility, drove on without slackening the speed, but Heather shifted uneasily in her seat.

"I always thought of New Mexico as being so dry. Is this storm a usual occurrence?"

"Sure is, in summer. At this altitude we may get one every afternoon. They're like mountain monsoons. It may even be snow higher up where we're headed."

Heather decided Betty must be warming up with the gratification a native feels in explaining local phenomena to a foreigner.

"In August? Do you get snow at the ranch?" Heather thought about the swimsuit and the light summer clothes she had packed.

"Sure. It can snow any time. It won't last long in summer, though. As soon as the sun comes out it's gone. And the nights are cold, but it's still warm in the daytime."

The next turn brought them onto a gravel road which became increasingly tortuous. Cottonwoods gave way to piñon and juniper. Then there were ponderosa pines and slim aspens. It was as green as Illinois or Wisconsin. The rain stopped suddenly, but clouds of vapor rose on the hillsides. They were really in the clouds! The mist on the green hillsides writhed upward like smoke, revealing distant canyons and steep gorges. Each turn of the road presented grander vistas and more precipitous cliffs.

Betty pulled the car off onto a narrow overlook turnout, parked, and pointed toward the north. "There's your Adobe Castle."

It was several moments before Heather could spot the tiny tower in the distance. She felt like the questing knight in *Idylls of the King*, seeing Tennyson's Camelot as it appeared and disappeared in the mist.

"But it's not adobe. It looks more like a Victorian mansion."

Betty's reply was one of icy archness. "The whole thing is a mishmash of additions. Part of it is adobe. Spanish walls, Indian ovens. Pretty much a jumble."

"It looks wonderful from here. I'm eager to see it all. And to find out if I still have a room reserved there. They must cater to reclusive clients who want to remain out of phone contact."

"I heard it was sold last year. You may want to stay at the Lazy-A. We have room, if you can't check in at the Castle."

Heather's heart sank at the thought. She could

not afford another large dent in her bank account. Her grandfather had agreed to her trip partly because it would take no more money out of her trust fund. "If anyone is there, I'm sure they'll honor my travel voucher. I don't need first-class accommodations. Let's see if it's open."

The last few miles of road were steeper and narrower. The Castle was hidden from view, and except for a sign marking the boundary of the Santa Fe National Forest, the surroundings were wilderness. Betty, looking doubtful, stopped the car at their last turnoff. A narrow lane descended steeply from the gravel road and looked impassable.

"I'm not sure about taking this car through those ruts," she said. "It's pretty low slung, not a good off-road vehicle."

With the sun gone behind the nearby mountain, the shade had brought a pseudo-dusk under the trees that belied the light of the sky overhead. Heather peered into the shadows. "Do I see a light through the trees? I can walk there from here." She wrenched her bag out of the back seat and added, "I'm sure I can make it. Let me pay you."

"No thanks. Glad to help." Betty's farewell was peremptory and her departure surprisingly abrupt.

Heather stood alone under the tall ponderosas. The silence was stirred first by a whisper of breeze in the treetops, then by the half whine, half yelp of a distant coyote. The rain-washed air felt crisp and fresh, redolent of pine and matted needles on the forest floor. But the gathering dusk of late afternoon brought a gloom that was too early and too deep to bolster the bravado she tried to muster as she started down the darkening lane.

Chapter II

Fortune favors the bold.

—Virgil

The distance to the Adobe Castle was greater than she had imagined. The light she had seen through the trees proved to be sunlight shining through a cleft in the canyon wall into a clearing in the forest. The shafts of sunlight were vanishing even as she approached. The darkening understory of the pines made the trail a fearsome path into the unknown. Why had Betty, knowing how far it must be, let her start out alone? Then she recalled her own determined and precipitate reply to Betty's offer of lodging. She must now prove to be as fearless as she was independent and cease feeling like Snow White fleeing in the forest of grotesque trees.

Her thoughts returned to her big plan. Even in her imagined scenario the thought of blood was repulsive. Maybe she should use poison. It would be less messy, and no one need be present at the victim's demise. But how could someone who was hesitant to walk in a strange forest attempt to plan a murder, let alone imagine its effect on others?

The suitcase seemed heavier. The wheels had become clogged with dirt after the first few yards of the trail, and she was forced to carry it. Fatigue added to her apprehension. Then she spied a break in the trees ahead.

The clearing opened on an unforgettable vista. To the east the heights dropped away to mesas unfolding from mesas, down to a river valley backed by a range of snow capped mountains. The blue distance became a shadow which moved up toward the white crest as the earth turned away from the sun. The snow turned pink, painted by the last rays, and then muted to lavender and gray as the shadow climbed inexorably upward.

She stared in disbelief. The beauty of the grand expanse was breathtaking and seemed almost unreal. She was watching the end of a surreal film with over-enhanced color.

She turned toward the western side of the clearing and decided she had been thrust into the pages of an old fashioned gothic novel. For there was the Adobe Castle, dark, imposing, and much larger than she had judged from a distance. The sunset sky behind the one Victorian tower created a silhouette that justified the Castle appellation, and the lower outlines of the sprawling two-story adobe structure gave the impression of a domestic fortress, solid and impregnable. Iron gratings on the windows were a lacy and exotic decoration as well as a reassurance of security.

Heather felt as if she were inside all the romance stories she had ever read. She was the new Mrs. De Winter approaching Rebecca's Manderley. She was Jane Eyre with her first look at Thornfield. She was Roderick's friend coming upon the melancholy House of Usher. Now, of course, a full moon should rise to complete the scene, she thought. Deciding not to wait for that final touch, she headed for the massive door beyond the low wall where the driveway ended. One window near the door shone with a dull light, but the rest of the Castle was dark.

A movement beyond the wall caught her attention and she thought she could see a dark figure slipping around the corner of the wall through a far gateway. Then she jumped aside, startled by a sudden movement on the path beside her. The dark shape became an animal which ran ahead of her toward the door.

She wondered if the big brass knocker on the door would now turn into the head of Scrooge's dead partner in *A Christmas Carol*.

But the knocker felt solid and real, and its banging brought a quick response. The door opened and the two people stood looking at each other in stunned surprise. Facing Heather was a woman in a tattered pink robe, holding a kerosene lamp. Her gray hair stuck straight out on the sides of her head. A huge pink roller held her top hair in a gigantic sausage curl. Her eyes were wide with wonder.

"Land sakes! Where did you come from? I didn't hear a car."

"I have a reservation—"

"I was afraid of that. And I'll bet you never got a cancelation. Affairs here are in a real mess. Well, come on in. I can't get you another hotel until tomorrow. Our power is out, and we don't even have the phone hooked up. Don Diego will be back tomorrow. Do you mind camping for one night?"

She rattled on with a long explanation of how Don Diego Ramirez had purchased the estate, had struggled to get a clear title, settled the unpaid utility bills while ownership was in limbo, and had become swamped with paperwork stacked in the study with a hodgepodge of unanswered correspondence, amidst which was probably Heather's reservation. While she talked, she led Heather into a huge kitchen with beamed ceiling. An open fireplace and a wood range radiated heat, and a spicy smell reminded her how hungry she was.

"You walked all the way from the road? My land, you must be starved. I have this posole and some Indian bread. Sit right here. I'm Mattie Higgins."

Heather introduced herself and sat down at the long plank table. The kerosene lamp made a warm circle of light, and the gray animal which had bounded ahead of her turned out to be a huge cat, which was now perched on the top of the cupboard and looking down at them with an aristocratic air. The stew was so spicy it burned her mouth, but by alternating tastes of it with bites of bread and sips of coffee she managed to satisfy her hunger without interrupting the cook's tale. Mattie, who was also the managing housekeeper, was not related to Diego Ramirez, but had worked for the previous owners and had been persuaded to stay at the Castle by an attractive increase in her stipend.

"Is his last name Diego?" Heather asked. "I thought you said it was Ramirez."

"It is Ramirez. Don is not for Donald. It's a Spanish title of respect, but he's lucky to get me to use the term. Señor Don Diego Ramirez is the big lord of the manor, you know, and expects to be treated that way, like a real Spanish grandee. Takes all his meals in the dining room. Expects me to say 'Yes Sir' and run this big old hotel like a private home with no dust. If he'd let me get into that study to sort out some of his papers, he'd be better off. He's an expert at lording it in the old fashioned way and has begun decorating with some fancy changes to make it look historical, but there's not one practical bone in his body. This place will never be a success until he gets a decent manager. But as long as I get my pay and time off to visit my daughter in Santa Fe each week, I'll stay on."

Heather explained her own desire to break free from a domineering grandfather who expected her to become a teacher, a profession she felt she wasn't suited for. She loved the literature she had studied in college and wanted to write, but in order to delay her inevitable employment in the classroom and to continue her writing, she had chosen to enter graduate school. Her grandfather would support her from her parents' trust fund only as long as she was in school.

"I don't mind staying here without the electricity. Do you think Señor Ramirez will approve?"

"It's not just the power. Even bathroom facilities are back to primitive. At least for tonight. If the power comes on tomorrow, the water pumps will work again, and it'll be a little nicer here. You can sleep in the Pueblo Room. Don Diego would want me to light a fire in there, so I'll do just that."

When she returned, she drew a pail of hot water from the tank at the end of the wood range, handed Heather a flashlight, and led her down a long hall to a white-walled room containing a huge bed. The down coverlet was patterned with a blue bear-symbol design. A white ewer and basin stood on a low table. Mattie poured water into the basin, showed her the towels, and pointed to the ceramic vessel under the bed. "These old fashioned room decorations come in handy when you have to live like a hundred years ago. Will you be okay?"

"This looks wonderful. Thanks. It's been a long trip, and I'm glad to have a bed."

Heather looked out the small window to the east. There it was. The moonrise! It wasn't the perfect full moon appropriate for this romantic setting, but a lopsided, waning gibbous moon, already past full. Still, it was huge on the horizon, and as it edged upward, it silhouetted the long line of the mountains against the sky and reminded her of the vastness of the landscape.

"Close enough," she sighed contentedly, and crawling under the warm comforter, fell asleep long before the piñon wood in the little fireplace turned to ashes.

Chapter III

When angry, count to four;
when very angry, swear.

–MARK TWAIN

Heather woke early. The room was still dark
and quite cold, but she could see the eastern sky
beginning to show behind the jagged horizon of
mountains. A morning star, far brighter than any
she had ever seen in the Midwest, was stabbing
the velvet blue with scintillating light. She had
to watch it for several moments before deciding
it really wasn't a plane or a weather balloon.
Then remembering delightedly that she was on
vacation, she turned again to sleep.

When she next woke, bright sunlight and the sound of birds called her to exercise. At home she enjoyed jogging early in the quiet suburban streets. Here, her run would be a delightful exploration of nature. Shorts and a T-shirt seemed to be scanty attire, but she knew anything heavier would feel too warm after she ran the first mile, except for her cold hands. She found a pair of white tube socks, and pulling them on as elbow-length mittens, started out down the trail behind the castle.

The trail led to a mountain stream where it made a T-junction. She decided to run upstream to explore the area back of the castle and attain the view that higher ground would give. But the rocky, uneven terrain forced her to focus her eyes on the path, and she soon found herself running parallel to the lane she had traveled the night before. The high altitude caused her breathing to become more deep and labored, and she was forced to alternate between jogging and walking, but the slower pace enhanced her enjoyment of the silent cathedral-like pine forest. The trail joined the Castle lane, then rose sharply to junction with the road. Pumping her arms, she released an extra burst of speed to attain the top of the rise, and in doing so nearly collided with a horse and rider.

The horse, startled by the waving white arms of the strange creature emerging from the shadows, reared suddenly and dumped his rider on the ground. Then he snorted, wheeled around, and galloped in panic down the road.

Horrified, she ran toward the sprawled horseman. "I'm sorry! I think I frightened your horse. Are you all right?"

He was muttering epithets and turning slowly to extricate his leg from an unnatural position. "Dammit! Can't you watch what you're doing?"

As she retrieved his cap which had landed several feet away, she saw the Du Von Films logo on it and realized that the unfortunate rider was the van driver from the Lamy station encounter.

Still uttering profanities softly, he pulled himself to a sitting position and resting his arms on his knees, looked up to examine the leggy wood nymph who was approaching him holding his cap in one hand and a pair of long white socks in the other. Part of her dark hair was pulled back from her face, but a few tendrils curled around her forehead which shone with perspiration.

Then he recognized her. "It's the lost princess. Did you find your castle?"

"Yes. It was well hidden, but I found it. But in going out to explore my kingdom, I didn't realize

I'd be facing mounted knights who had no armor."

"Not even proper boots, which would've helped. I think I twisted an ankle." Heather tried to assist him as he struggled to his feet and applied weight gingerly to his left leg. "I'm staying at the Lazy-A. Maybe they'll come looking for me when they see the horse coming back without me."

"I can get help at the Adobe Castle. It's down this lane. Do you think you can walk at all?"

"I think I can get going here in a minute. Give me a shoulder prop." He leaned on Heather and began a tentative limping walk.

Their progress was painfully slow. With each step his face came close to hers, close enough for her to feel his breath by her hair. He was trying to keep the pressure of his hand from being too heavy on her shoulder. Was he really in that much pain?

Deciding on a more expedient course of action, she stopped and turned to him with a suggestion. "You really should probably elevate your foot. There's a stream near here. I'll go soak these socks to wrap around your ankle. Then while you rest, I'll run back to the Castle and get help."

When she returned from the stream, she experienced a pang of guilt at her surmise that he had been exaggerating his discomfort. He had removed his shoe and sock, and she could see that the ankle was already swollen and red. Their hands fumbled together as she wrapped it in the dripping socks.

Grabbing her hands, he said, "Here, dry your hands on my shirt. That's really ice water, and your hands must be frozen." He held her cold hands on his chest, under his own warm hands, which were surprisingly large and strong.

Their eyes met and she smiled briefly. Then slowly pulling away, she started down the trail toward the Castle. I can't plan a murder plot, she thought, when I keep finding myself inside a romance novel. She realized she had almost rehearsed a parody of the scene in *Jane Eyre* where Mr. Rochester fell as his horse slipped near the gate and Jane had helped him up.

Except Mr. Rochester was not supposed to be so handsome, she mused, thinking of the injured Brian.

Her thoughts were interrupted by the sound of a car or truck. She ran back to the lane, hoping to wave it down and enlist help. But when she returned to the spot where she had left him, she found that Brian was already gone. A low haze of dust from the vehicle hung over the lane and one wet sock lay on the ground.

She experienced a confusion of feeling. There was an appropriate gratification that he had been rescued, but there was also a strange disappointment that she could no longer be of any help. She picked up the sock and jogged slowly back toward the Castle.

Chapter IV

But he spake no word;
which set the horror higher.

—ALFRED, LORD TENNYSON

Brian had settled against a big ponderosa pine to wait for Heather's return. The bark, rough with big orange scales, had a vanilla aroma, and the entire forest smelled spicy clean. But he marveled at how yesterday's rain had left no mud, and the sun in the clear patches showed the road was already dry and dusty.

Being site-coordinator for a film company was turning out to be more of a job than he had bargained for. Since his father had turned him loose with his investment fund and then turned against him when he revealed he was sinking it into a "fly-by-night movie outfit," Brian had alternated with the feeling that movie-making in New Mexico would bring a sure profit and the doubt that the adventure would overbalance the hassles. His degree in business from Michigan State did not qualify him for cinematography. But when Pierre Du Von had explained what investing in Southwest filming would be like, Brian decided it could be an interesting and speedy way to multiply his money.

He had decided that his current assignment, that of finding a suitable outdoor locale for the film in progress, at a site close enough to housing for the cast and crew, was not going to be as simple as he had thought. While the company were finishing the indoor shots at the studios in Santa Fe, he had checked in at the Lazy-A Dude Ranch to scout for an open and scenic site for the outdoor footage. He cursed himself for trying to play cowboy and explore the area on horseback instead of driving. But the Bergens, owners of the Lazy-A, had told him that the most scenic trails and open overlooks were not accessible by car, and a horse from the Lazy-A stables seemed the proper choice. He wished now that he'd tried to rent a mountain bike instead.

And, he recalled, he had promised himself that females were not going to mess up his plans again. After the little blonde vixen who worked next to him had cost him his job at General Motors, he had sworn off women with their conniving, cutesy wiles. And now, here he was stranded with a morning wasted because a jogging princess had come charging out of the woods. He was struck by her elfin beauty and the dimple that showed in one cheek when she smiled. But even as he recalled her slim hands on his chest and her apologetic attempt to rescue him, he vowed he would not be tempted to pursue the acquaintance further. There was a mysterious air of self-possession about her and a reticent self-containment that intrigued him, but while he admitted he was curious to know more about her, he disliked the aura of quiet superiority that she seemed to display.

His musings were interrupted by the sound of a pickup truck speeding toward him down the lane. Big wheels held the chrome and red cab high off the road, and the roar of the engine signified more horsepower than the winding path required. When the driver spied Brian sitting beside the lane with his white-wrapped ankle, he braked and backed to him, opening the door for a closer look. Brian struggled to his feet and grabbed the door handle. The driver was a middle-aged dark-skinned man wearing sunglasses that concealed his eyes, and a wide red headband that held down his long straight black hair which ended in a pigtail.

His face remained impassive, and because he said nothing, Brian spoke first. "Headed toward the Adobe Castle? Mind if I ride along? Had a little upset and lost my horse."

The dark man didn't reply, but his slow nod seemed as much invitation as Brian needed, so he climbed in and fastened the seatbelt. As the truck got underway, Brian volunteered his name and other details that explained how he came to be sitting alone in the forest with a wet sock around his ankle. But the driver stared straight ahead and drove in silence, one muscular arm across the top of the steering wheel and a massive right hand bearing an eagle-head ring resting on the gearshift.

Brian had always guarded against stereotyping at first meeting, but here was the actual picture of a stoic Indian. The high cheekbones, Roman nose, and stolid demeanor reinforced all his movie images of the native Red Man, and the dark skin, dark glasses, and silence emphasized the impression of implacable and mysterious power. His presence, Brian admitted to himself, was definitely intimidating, and, disliking the reticence most of all, he tried to pry some words from him by making further inquiries.

"Do you live near here?"

The dark man kept his eyes on the road, but nodded slowly.

"I'm Brian Minter, with Du Von Films. You are—?"

"Sam Redfox, Santa Inés Pueblo." The reply was slow, but the words were clipped with sharp pauses between them.

Encouraged at eliciting a reply, Brian tried again. "I'm looking for a scenic open area for some scenes in a film. Do you know of any near here?"

There was no reply, but the truck began to slow down. He didn't know if Redfox was slowing in anticipation of rough road ahead, because they were nearing their destination, or if he were about to be roughed up, robbed, and left in the woods. He recalled the time he had been mugged in Detroit, and he now wondered at his own naiveté in climbing into a vehicle with a strange man in a strange forest in this Rocky Mountain wilderness. His breathing quickened as he reached for the seatbelt release and the door handle. But as they rounded the next sharp turn, he realized the stop was the answer to his last question because the open meadow he now saw included the overlook of the valley view with the descending mesa tops backed by the Sangre de Cristo Mountains. The beauty of the vast panorama struck him into a silence that matched that of his driver. He exhaled in relief and wonderment. Then as he turned to see the sprawling adobe structure and the Victorian tower on the other side of the meadow, he smiled in gratification. He had found what he'd been looking for.

"Is this the Adobe Castle? Where can I ask about housing for a film crew?"

Again Redfox maintained his silence but slowly lifted his arm and pointed at the castle, then proceeded to drive toward the gate in the adobe wall.

Brian climbed down and limped through the gateway toward the massive door. He waited for what seemed like a long time before the sound of the heavy knocker brought a response. The red-faced housekeeper was wiping her hands on her ample-hipped jeans as if interrupted in culinary pursuits to answer the door. "Have a seat here while I inquire if Don Diego is receiving anyone yet."

"Receiving anyone? Isn't this a hotel? I want to ask about housing for about thirty people." But hearing he was in such a formal situation, he decided he could match the formality with corresponding etiquette. Taking a Du Von Films business card from his shirt pocket, he gave it to the housekeeper with a slight bow, and said, "Brian

Minter is calling to request an interview with the lord of the manor regarding accommodations for several guests of the Du Von Company."

She took the card with a sneer at his sarcasm and swept out, shutting the hall door with a firmness that was just short of a slam.

Five minutes later she returned with a card on a tray. The card was the size of a playing card and bore in ornate lettering the engraved name of Don Diego Ramirez followed by a message written in a bold hand with black ink, "Requests the pleasure of your company at seven tonight for dinner and the discussion of any business."

The housekeeper smiled smugly at her one-up manship in the duel of formality and added, "Sam will take you back to your hotel. Let him know if you need a ride back here tonight."

Left speechless for the second time, Brian conceded that a silent acquiescence would be the most noble response, so he bowed as low as he could, sweeping his cap across his feet, then walked in as dignified a manner as his limp would allow back toward the waiting truck.

A big gray cat coming toward him near the gate eyed him archly then turned abruptly, and with tail and head held high, strode slowly away.

Chapter V

*Ghost, n. The outward and visible sign
of an inward fear.*

—AMBROSE BIERCE

Heather, returning from her run, came through the back gate of the Castle and found Mattie busy at both stoves in the kitchen, her face reddened with the heat from the range, and smiling pleasantly as she told the news that the electric power had been restored.

"Now you can have your shower, and I can get dinner organized for Don Diego and his snooty guest. You'll finally get to meet your grand host and see how he likes to run his dining room."

"Who is the other guest?" Heather poured a glass of water and sat at the oilcloth table.

"Fellow in sneakers and denim suit wanting rooms for a film company."

"Was he limping? How did he get here?" After hearing Mattie's explanation and relating her own encounter with Brian, she was eager to meet the host who had dealt so formally with the unlucky rider.

"You won't meet him until dinner at seven. He's busy with the business papers that keep him so riled up. He gave strict orders that he is not to be disturbed. But he was not happy about me giving you the Pueblo Room. He wants to move you into the Tower Room."

"Was the Pueblo Room already reserved for someone else?"

"No, but he says the Tower is more appropriate for a single lady guest. I said I'd ask you about changing rooms, but he was pretty set on having me just tell you that it was necessary for you to move up there. He doesn't consider the extra work involved for me, of course. Or the fact that you'd have to climb three flights of stairs."

"I don't mind stairs, especially if there's a good view. May I go up and see the room?"

Mattie stopped chopping vegetables and dried her hands. She took a huge key from the window shelf. "Let me turn down the heat under this rice, and I'll show you up."

"No, I won't interrupt your cooking. Doesn't the long hall connect directly with the other part of the hotel? I think I can find my way up there." And taking the key, she left before Mattie could object.

Passing from the adobe hallway into the Victorian passageway, she sensed an abrupt change. Even though the adobe structure was older, its smooth light walls and beamed ceilings gave it a modern and efficient firmness that was a contrast to the board floors, the figured wallpaper, and the dark furniture of the wooden structure. She passed through an attractively furnished dining room, noting that the wide boards of the floor, though clean and polished, creaked as she walked across them.

The stairway to the tower was not circular, but the balustrades ended in ornately carved newel posts, and the two landings were decorated with large blue and white urns filled with ferns. At the top of the last flight she fitted the key into a large keyhole where it turned easily, but she had trouble pushing the door open. Having been recently varnished, the door edges were sticking, she guessed.

But the room inside was a delight. She entered a suite of antique splendor with decor and furnishings making it fit for royalty. The monstrous canopied bed was hung with filmy draperies, the overstuffed blue chairs and velvet-covered chaise were decorated with ivory satin pillows, and the adjoining bathroom featured gold-rimmed sinks fitted into ornate tables. The abundance of tassels and fringes was almost theatrical, but the combination of lace, shades of blue, and dark wood, created an ambience that was plush without being decadently opulent. The room was definitely a tribute to Don Diego's skill in interior decorating, and her reassignment there a compliment to her as his first guest.

On the west wall antique portraits in oval gilt frames hung between lace-curtained windows, but the east wall showed her the magnificent view of the valley through a much larger window than that of the Pueblo Room. She ran downstairs to gather up her clothes and inform Mattie that she was moving into the tower.

After her shower she finished unpacking and opened the high armoire to hang up some blouses. The inside surface of the armoire door was a tall mirror. When she turned to glance into it before closing the door, she stopped short and ceased breathing. A man in a dark uniform was standing behind her in the middle of the room, his face reflected above hers in the glass.

She turned to face him, but saw no one there. She felt faint and her knees went weak. When she caught her breath again she managed to speak. "Hello? Is there someone here?" She forced herself to walk back to the door. Opening it, she saw only the empty staircase.

She sat on the edge of the bed till her heart-beat slowed down and some strength returned to her legs. Then she looked into the mirror again, but saw only her own large dark eyes in a face pale with fright.

Still trembling, she headed down to the adobe kitchen where Mattie was bustling amid the spicy vapors of her own concoctions. "Do you like the fancy room? What's the matter? You're shaking. You look like you've seen a ghost."

"I have." And she explained how the strange vision had appeared.

"Nonsense! One of those movie actors probably arrived early and started exploring through the rooms. I'll come up and look."

Heather followed as Mattie climbed the three flights to arrive puffing with exertion. After she looked around the suite, she opened and closed the armoire. Then she opened it again and began to laugh. "Look here. Here's your ghost. You're seeing the old man in the picture on the far wall. With the door at this angle, he's reflected twice, once from the dressing table mirror and then back to this one."

And she swung the door to catch the image for Heather's view of it. "You're moving too fast and getting too excited. Running five miles before breakfast when you're not used to this altitude would make anyone see things. Come on down and get something to eat before you faint away on me."

"Maybe you're right," Heather replied meekly. As she followed Mattie out of the room past the wall portrait, she noted more carefully the bushy mustache, clean chin and high forehead of the bald old gentleman in the antique frame. He was not the intruder she had seen in the mirror.

The man she had seen in the reflection was bearded, with a profusion of blond hair hanging over his youthful forehead.

Chapter VI

Charm is a product of the unexpected.

—JOSE MARTI

"Don Diego expects everyone to dress for dinner," Mattie explained. "And that smart-alec movie man will probably make a fool of himself, thinking he'll impress him."

"I brought only one dress," Heather complained. "And it's not very formal."

"Is it black? He likes black. If it's a dark color, it'll look fine." Mattie was going in and out of the kitchen taking silver from a carved cupboard to set the dining table.

Heather remembered she did have one black dress that wasn't really a dress. It was a pool sarong, made of terry cloth velour which could pass for velveteen in a dim light.

Trying to forget that she'd seen an apparition, she stood in front of the mirror in the tower room, surveying her reflection. Adjusting the black belt on the long robe, she noticed that the straight cut of the garment clung to her figure in very flattering lines and that the concealing high neckline was balanced by the daring slit up one leg. Turning sideways, she pulled her hair up and decided that having it piled atop her head would make a more formal coiffure.

The tall Spanish clock in the hallway was striking seven as she walked into the library that adjoined the dining room. Brian Minter had already arrived and was waiting in a big leather chair near the fireplace. He rose as Heather entered and gave a low whistle of admiration. "The fair princess! You have wounded me, and now you will make me your captive."

"And how is your ankle?" She smiled at his attempt at pleasant blarney, but remained coolly composed, at least outwardly. He was dressed formally, and although the black suit was not well cut, his broad shoulders gave it a tailored appearance, and his ruddy tan contrasted healthily with the white shirt front. He carried a cane, and only the bandaged ankle and loose sandals detracted from the complete picture of a Byronic hero.

"My ankle is improving rapidly," he said, "especially since I've sworn off horses."

He broke off suddenly at seeing his host enter the room. "Mr. Ramirez! Hello. I'm Brian Minter. I appreciate your invitation." He limped forward, extending his hand.

Don Diego Ramirez paused in the doorway to the library. He presented an imposing figure: tall and imperially slim with iron-gray hair, dark eyes and handsome classic features. His dark gray suit was of a western cut accented by a black bolo tie with a miniature silver escutcheon. He would certainly flutter the pulses on the Santa Fe streets, Heather thought. The only feature not in keeping with a slick menswear model was the heavy eyebrows which gave his face a severe expression, and the only touch of vanity in an otherwise conservative appearance was his silver-toed boots.

He shook Brian's hand warmly but immediately directed his attention to Heather. Bowing low he said, "Miss McMarley! I am charmed to meet you. Welcome to the Adobe Castle and accept my apologies for the difficulties you experienced in arriving here. Also for your poor accommodations the first night. Is the Tower Room satisfactory?" His voice was smooth and deep, and the hint of a Spanish accent added to the charm of his greeting.

Heather assured him she had not been inconvenienced by any of the arrangements, praised the decor of the Tower Room, and expressed gratitude for Mattie's help. "But as long as I'm the only guest, wouldn't it be better if I stayed in the Pueblo Room? I hate to inconvenience the help by having them go up there to make up the room."

He assured her that she was not to consider her hosts inconvenienced in any way, and dismissing the subject summarily, he tucked her hand inside his arm and escorted her into the dining room. "I have found your reservation in my hopeless pile of documents. Had it not been misplaced, your arrival could have been much easier. I note that your middle name on the voucher is Luna. Are you Spanish?"

"My mother was Spanish. My father, Irish."

"A fortunate combination. You have inherited the beauty of both races." Whether due to the hospitality he felt he owed his first guest, the bias he felt in favor of Castillian heritage, or her attractiveness, he focused all of his attention on Heather, largely ignoring Brian. He seated her on his right at the massive dining table, himself at the head, Brian across from her on his left. The gray cat followed them into the dining room, leaped to the top of the china cabinet, and sat at attention, presiding over the diners.

Mattie bustled in and out of the dining room, bringing steaming plates of enchiladas. "I put the green chile on the side for you, Heather. But you'll soon get to like our New Mexico style," she added.

Don Diego glared silently at Mattie. The dining room with its beamed ceiling and white walls, the massive furniture of dark polished wood, the candlelight reflecting on the silver bowls and on the faces of the formal diners, all gave an elegant and refined grace to the meal, in contrast to which Mattie produced a brash and discordant note. Her loud clumping steps, brisk chatter, red smiling face, and blue-jeaned informality jarred on Don Diego's sensibilities and spoiled the effect he had intended for his guests.

Heather could sense his dark disapproval and smiled inwardly at Mattie's actions, which she felt were purposely at odds with the class distinction Don Diego wanted to preserve between master and servant.

After Mattie had left the room, Don Diego became a genial host, warming expansively with comments about his plans for further improvements on the Adobe Castle. Suddenly remembering a message for his guest, he informed her that her grandfather had called, worried because the establishment had been out of phone contact until today. "But I assured him that you had arrived, that all is fine, and that he is not to worry. We are like a family here, and I am not known as Tio Diego for nothing, eh? Tio Diego means Uncle Jim, that's who I am." And smiling, he laid his hand on top of hers.

Heather was a little miffed at being given her message as an afterthought instead of being called to the phone. And she disliked being put in the position of the little girl who needed to be protected, instead of that of an independent woman traveling on her own. At the same time she did feel some distrust of this lord of the manor. His smile was not as reassuring as his words intended, and the way he kept his hand with its massive silver crest ring on hers was more than avuncular. She reddened and withdrew it slowly from beneath his.

"Try the sopaipillas. Are you not familiar with these? Put some honey inside. Very delicious." He offered the basket, which contained the little deep-fried hollow pastries to Heather, then to Brian.

"Sofa pillows?" Brian and Heather said the words in unison, looked at each other and laughed. The New Mexican pastry did resemble little pillows, and the similarity had struck them at the same time. Brian leaned forward, his elbow on the table, and offered his little finger, inviting Heather's response. She likewise reached out and hooked her little finger into his, and they both repeated, "Needles and pins. My wish wins," before laughing again and unhooking their hands.

Because Don Diego frowned uncomprehendingly, Brian explained that it was a childhood custom to make a wish when the same thought occurred to two people at the same time.

He nodded in acknowledgement, but the severe expression on his face betrayed the fact that he felt excluded from the shared joke and disapproved of the warmth of the look the two younger people had shared. The conversation faltered and they continued eating in silence until Mattie's heavy tread intruded as she brought the dessert, sunshine flan, a smooth delicious custard to end the meal.

The gray cat leaped down from the china cabinet and jumped onto the chair at the foot of the table to sit with his chin just above the table edge, staring at Don Diego.

"You forgot to set a place for him," laughed Heather. "I think he wants some dessert."

"He knows his place," said Don Diego. "He also

knows he does not eat at the table."

"He's a smart cat, then, or intelligent enough to be well trained," added Brian.

Don Diego shifted in his chair as if to straighten his rigid posture, brushed an imaginary crumb from the tablecloth with the back of his little finger, and explained, "He is a British shorthair, from a very good line. His sire is Duke Block, and his mother is Bluestocking, from the Essex line. Therefore his name is Blue Chip, but he is called Chipper for short.

"A valuable chip off the old block, then?" laughed Brian.

"And now, my Dear," Don Diego said with an air of decisive finality, "you must excuse us gentlemen while we retreat to our cigars and brandy. I will escort you to the library where we will return shortly to join you for coffee. Come, Mr. Minter, we shall discuss the arrangements we spoke of earlier."

Now Heather was the one to feel excluded. Would she have felt less so had there been other women dining with them? This after-dinner ritual was in keeping with the customs followed in an old romantic comedy of manners. But she felt she may still prefer a modern story in which courtesy is based on a closer equality of the sexes. She picked up the gray cat which had followed them to the library and chose the leather chair by the fireplace in which to wait for the gentlemen.

The cat struggled free from her grasp and jumping down, stalked away with his tail twitching, showing his disgust at her familiarity. He leaped onto the end table across from the chair, licked his chest as if adjusting his vest, and fixed Heather with an arrogant stare.

Heather smiled and said to him, "So I've offended your dignity. I apologize. You're not a lap cat, I see. I won't try to hold you. But we can remain friends and try to understand each other."

She had read somewhere that cats connect with humans through long stares, interrupted by blinks. Holding her gaze on his yellow eyes, she sensed the mystery of his feline ancestry, the power of ancient Egypt where cats were gods, the strength of the jungle where cats were kings, and the magic of witchcraft in which cats were the familiars of the agents of evil.

She slowly closed her eyes and opened them again. The gray cat responded with the same slow blink. They seemed in tune with each other.

Relaxed and determined, she decided she would insist on having her room changed back to the adobe wing. Even though her stay was a prize gift, she was still the customer, and the customer has a right to choose her accommodations. She would not be a wimp.

After what seemed like an inordinate length of time, Don Diego and Brian returned. With a bow and apologies for the delay, Don Diego called for coffee and before Heather could bring up the matter, he explained that all the rooms were now reserved because he had concluded the arrangements with Du Von Films to accommodate the cast and crew, beginning tomorrow, at the Adobe Castle. Over coffee he explained that he would be hiring girls from the nearby Santa Inés Pueblo to serve as chamber maids and that Heather was not to think of moving from the guest-of-honor room in the tower.

Unable to think of a logical objection, Heather decided that she had no alternative but to acquiesce gracefully and that she would prove herself less of a wimp by facing the haunted tower than by insisting on her rights as the first lodger.

"A tower room is an appropriate place for a princess," Brian said. "But perhaps the authenticity of your aristocracy may be questioned. You'd better look to see if there is a small vegetable of any kind underneath the mattress. Or maybe the room is haunted. Don't ghosts like to hang out in towers?"

Her goodnight was given with a rather cool tone. Don Diego extended his hand, which she took briefly, but she turned away stiffly as Brian also extended his. The gray cat seemed to sense the military determination of her demeanor and marched ahead of her up the stairs as if leading her to a dangerous but unavoidable assignation.

Chapter VII

Night brings our troubles to the light,
rather than banishes them.

—Lucius, Annaeus Seneca

After she entered the tower room and turned on the lights, Heather hesitated in the doorway, surveying the elegant and shadowy room. The wall switch was connected only to the low lamps on the bureau and on the bedside cabinet, but the farthest corners of the room remained in darkness. She felt a cold wave of air, and her apprehension, aided by an imaginative memory, held her immobile.

One sign of a ghostly presence, she recalled, is a chilling wave of air. What was the other sign? Oh, yes, a burning candle will go dim. She remembered the line from Shakespeare, "How ill this taper burns!" Maybe I should light a candle, she mused.

She was brought back to reality when Chippercat, who was roaming the room as if doing his own spirit search, batted the moving hem of the floor-length drapery near the window. She laughed at herself as she added up: moving curtain, open window, open door, draught. Close the door and lock it, Silly, and stop being paranoid.

After sniffing the corners and investigating all the furniture legs, Chipper jumped onto the bed and proceeded to wash his face and ears, confidently choosing his berth for the night.

Heather made short work of her own ablutions with the rationalization that the faster she could get into bed, the more quickly she'd feel warm again. Her haste really precluded opening the armoire or looking into any mirrors.

Silken sheets and feather coverlet soon brought a cozy warmth and induced a deep and comforting sleep. But the soporific coziness did not ensure a long lasting rest. Strange dreams began to surface from the day's events. She found herself at the evening's formal dinner. Brian was holding her little finger again. She felt an electric thrill as he looked into her eyes. But suddenly he reached across to embrace her face with both hands. The blue gray cat jumped up onto the table and began eating the flan from her dish. Then Mattie walked into the room wearing a long strapless gown decorated with purple sequins and began laughing raucously at the destruction of decorum. Don Diego stood up shouting and pounding the table, his face distorted in anger.

The pounding faded but preceded her into waking consciousness as she awoke actually hearing repeated thuds. Footsteps? Someone was on the landing outside her door. Heart pounding, she turned onto her back and pushed the comforter away to listen. The sounds grew fainter as if the night walker were now descending the staircase. She held her breath until full silence reigned again. The waning gibbous moon had come across the sky to shine into the window, silvering all that it touched and revealing the cat still curled in sleep at the foot of the bed.

She couldn't decide if the footsteps had been only a part of her dream, a night watchman patrolling the castle, or the return of the apparition from the mirror. The swarming thoughts now whirled through her head with fully awakened awareness, bringing a litany of worries that had remained offstage during the day, but now played on the center stage of her consciousness while she sat watching helplessly, chained in a front row seat. She saw her grandfather repeating, "Even if you're twenty-one, you won't have your share of the trust until you marry or prove you're in a decent career. Your brother Robbie squandered his share on that car and God knows what else, and I'm still trying to make up the deficit."

She heard the Dean saying, " Here's an entry for the mystery story writing contest, Heather. You're a good writer, and if you place well in this contest, you'll cinch the grad-school acceptance with a fellowship and have a nice addition to your job résumé."

She heard her supervising teacher saying, "You'll never make a good teacher if you can't be more firm with the students."

The scenes with their importunate actors circulated two or three times until they ended with the high school classroom again, and she slid back into a troubled sleep, this time haunted by a first-class nightmare. She was standing at the front of the high school literature class and in terror realized that she was completely unprepared to teach the lesson. Her panic was augmented by the fact that she was wearing only a towel and trying to hold it up with one hand while holding the roll book with the other. The students not only refused to respond, but seemed completely unaware of her presence as they demolished the room. Some were hanging out the window calling to friends, some were standing on the desks and shouting, and some were chasing around the room, throwing books at each other. One boy was swinging from the light fixture, and as the fixture broke away from the ceiling, he landed in a pile of plaster and overturned chairs. Then a school counselor appeared in the doorway. She was a clown, wearing a beach hat decorated with an orange flower, a long dress covered with stars, and a necklace featuring a crescent moon pendant. She smiled at Heather acknowledging that the circus of animals is to be accepted as if beyond concern, nodded her head, touched the moon pendant, and floated away.

The scene evaporated and Heather woke, grateful to be back in the tower room, but wishing she could recall the clown lady to ask for help.

The moonlight had disappeared and the now darkened room began to echo with the sounds of distant thunder. It grew closer and with it came the sound of wind and rain. As the wind died, the rain pattering on the roof sounded a rhythm that lingered after the thunder had passed, and it lulled her back to a sleep undisturbed by further dreams.

Chapter VIII

No one our age should look that good.

—MARILYN DIENES

Bright morning sunlight dispersed the phantom dreams of the night and so cheerily illumined the tower room that Heather doubted the reality of the midnight footsteps.

She searched for her Nikes, looking forward to her morning run up the trail. Suddenly she stopped and was gripped by a horror of disbelief as she looked at the window. It was open.

The specters of darkness can be explained away in the sunshine, but anomalies in the daytime cannot be so easily dismissed. She stood wondering at first and repeated to herself, "I closed that window. I know I closed that window." Her trancelike self-questioning was interrupted by the small voice of Chipper standing at the door wanting out.

She decided that out was where she also wanted to be as soon as possible, and racing Chipper down the stairs, she headed for the back entrance and out into the sunshine.

Heading up the trail, she soon felt a change of air and found herself enveloped in fog. The sunshine was gone. After climbing up the trail she realized that she was actually in the clouds that had lingered from the rain, and after a few more switchbacks that left her breathless, she rounded a corner that brought her above the fog. She turned and gasped at the beauty of the panorama. She was again in the sunshine, looking out over a sea of clouds that concealed the trees and the castle below. She felt as if she were in the heavens, looking across miles of white ocean that shifted slowly as she watched. Finally she could see the top of the Castle tower, even though the rest of the building remained concealed. Starting down again, she felt the magical sense of being enveloped in shadowy fog once more and slowed her pace to accommodate the steep descent.

At the top of a long straight slant in the trail, she looked up to see a strange apparition. A woman, enveloped in a long gray gown like the fog was standing at the bottom of the hill. At first Heather doubted her senses or thought another tower ghost had finally manifested itself, pursuing her into the woods. As she came closer, she realized the woman was flesh and blood, and the gray form emerged as a pale blue cape, topped by a monstrous hat which was tied down with a green scarf.

She was holding a leash at the end of which a huge yellow cat was straining to sniff at the scrub oak beside the trail. The woman turned and smiled as Heather came down the trail. She was missing a tooth, and the lines around her smile showed her to be much older than she first appeared, but her eyes were bright, her complexion rosy, and she carried an air of graceful dignity that seemed at odds with her strange clothing, which bulged in what looked like several layers beneath the long cape, and hung at uneven lengths below it.

"Good morning! You're an early exerciser, I see. I'm Lola LaFey, wardrobe mistress, makeup lady, and holder of safety pins for the movie people. We are moving to the Castle to finish the filming, and I had a chance to ride over with the early group." She tucked a strand of auburn hair back under her hat and pulled her cape closer to her neck, fingering a large pendant. It was a silver crescent moon.

Heather was stunned at seeing the jewelry that replicated that of the clown lady in her dream, but she managed to blurt out a greeting to the stranger. "I thought you were a ghost until I saw the cat. The Adobe Castle is beautiful. You'll like it here. Unless," she added, "you get a haunted room. I think I have spirits in mine."

The cloaked lady picked up the yellow cat and joined Heather on the path back toward the Castle. "Sometimes old houses do have a presence that has lingered on. I will probably sense it if so. I have a gift of sensitivity, you know." She spoke with a confident serenity that made the supernatural seem as common as old wallpaper.

The yellow cat began squirming and they realized it had spotted Chipper, who was crouching as if to pounce at the newcomers.

"Calm down, Malkin. You can get acquainted after we settle in and get your leash off. We'll butter your toes as soon as we can find the cook. When a cat licks its feet," she explained, "it's inclined to feel the place is home."

"You'll find our cook if you go in at this back entrance. I'm going to take a cool-down walk outside the wall before going in."

Heather called to Chipper who, disgusted at the lack of an encounter, ran toward a huge adobe oven just inside the castle wall. The bee-hive-shaped structure looked as if it could be a big doghouse or a lawn mower shed. Chipper disappeared behind it and Heather headed down toward the front of the Castle, finally stopping by a ponderosa pine at the corner of the meadow in front of the Castle.

The stillness of the morning was broken by the sound of approaching cars and vans. Some were already parked near the entrance. As she leaned to stretch against a tree, she saw a man approaching carrying a travel bag in each hand. His insouciant stride, sharp good looks, and leather jacket all said Hollywood, and before he came much closer, she realized she was seeing Jack Hilton, the star of the cowboy movies she had watched as a child. But he seemed so short. She accepted that he looked older, but in her memory he had always been the long, lean, tall-in-the-saddle western hero, not this short, almost stocky man coming up the path.

When he spied her from a distance, his approving glance became a steadier gaze that moved down her torso, taking in her bare legs, and returning to her face with an approving smile. Brian, emerging from the Castle gate and facing the newcomer, followed the traveler's focused stare to see Heather standing by the tree. He waved at her and as he met Jack Hilton, extended his hand in greeting. Heather was too far away to catch all of their conversation, but as Jack set down his bags to meet Brian, she heard their laughter and guessed that the ageing movie star still had an eye for female forms because snatches of his comments were something about being pleased to move into a hotel that featured wood nymphs in the courtyard.

Jack disappeared inside the wall and Brian turned to walk toward the next arriving car, a taxi from Santa Fe. As Brian approached the taxi and opened the rear door with a welcome, nature seemed to conspire with Hollywood as the sun came from behind the clouds to spotlight the visitor for a grand entrance. Emerging from the car and standing up in one smooth and graceful move, was a goddess of the silver screen. The young woman was thin as a Barbie doll and tall, wearing a white dress that clung snugly from shoulders to waist and flared gracefully about her hips. Her blonde hair returned the sunlight in a coiffure that Prince Valiant's Aleta could have envied. From this distance it appeared like spun gold, soft as cotton candy, swept up and back toward a loose braid that hung over one shoulder. Her classic face with high cheekbones and ivory complexion invited closer scrutiny, and she stood with a calm demeanor that invited royal allegiance as if accustomed to the focus of many cameras. Like a model posing with a contra posta stance, she lifted her chin and looked slowly around the meadow while Brian paid the driver and began unloading her bags. If she saw Heather, she gave no indication, and if she was impressed by the sight of the huge castle, no one could tell from her cool expressionless glance. Heather suddenly felt like a scruffy animal in comparison to all this glamor and decided to return by the same outside circuit to the rear entrance of the castle. Brian, in dazed admiration of the dazzling princess, led her toward the front gate.

Chapter IX

*A disputant no more cares for the truth
than the sportsman for the hare.*

—ALEXANDER POPE

The smell of toast and bacon was a warm welcome to the castle kitchen where Mattie and Lola LaFey sat talking over coffee. The big yellow cat was sitting on a corner stool licking its paws and extending the procedure into a complete shampoo, rubbing a paw over the top of its head. Unlike an ordinary cat, the ears were folded forward and lay close to the head, giving it a rounded and babyish appearance. Heather knelt by the stool to examine the cat more closely.

"It's a Scottish Fold breed." explained Lola. "Banned from the British feline societies, but

very popular here. Maulkin is called a red mack-
erel tabby and could take prizes as best-of-show,
I'm sure. But her best feature is her sensitivity.
She can sense danger, oncoming storms, or people who are not to be trusted."

"They must think of you as a witch, then,"
laughed Heather. "And Malkin is your familiar,
your little devil's helper, so to speak."

Mattie's abrupt march to the stove for the coffee pot showed her disgusted dismissal of the
topic. She set a big coffee mug down, making a
place at the table for Heather and stood with
arms akimbo, looking at her.

"Could I bring Malkin up to my room in the
tower?" asked Heather. "I'd like to see if she
senses anything strange there."

Mattie could contain herself no longer and
exploded, "Why do you insist on all this spook
stuff about the Tower Room? Let me tell you, I'm
tired of all that nonsense. And let me tell you—
when the room was first refurnished, I slept
there myself, in order to see if there was any
truth to the silly stories being told. And there was
never a spook, or a rapping, or a wailing of any
kind in any way shape or form."

"Then you admit there have been stories
about the tower?" countered Heather. "I remembered the waitress at the Lamy restaurant telling

that the previous owners had trouble with ghosts."

"A bunch of nonsense. I think they were rumors started over at the Lazy-A by the Bergens, the couple who wanted to buy the Castle before Don Diego came. They probably thought they could scare away potential guests as well as any buyer also. There's no truth to any of it."

Lola fingered her pendant, straightened her shoulders and entered the argument. "A real ghost can actually add to the appeal of a hotel," she said. "People are curious, and I believe some would actually ask to sleep in a haunted room. And not everyone can feel the presence of a spirit. Some people really are more sensitive than others, you know." Her tone implied that Mattie's negative stance put her in the category of a coarse and unfeeling clod.

Mattie was about to condemn the witch lady with a scathing retort, when the door burst open and admitted a young man who fairly danced into the room asking, "How can I get some of that good coffee I smell? What a great kitchen! You can relax, Ladies. Mickey Lukey is here, your cook, caterer, and charming entertainer! What a great place for filming. The Adobe Castle! Whoever heard of such a far-out place as this? It'll be great."

To the amazement of the three women he continued to circle the kitchen, chattering and opening cupboard doors as he went. He was tall and thin, with red curly hair that was shaved closely on the sides of his head, but bounced in curls over his forehead. He was wearing a T-shirt that pictured a bearded long-haired man holding a money bag in each hand and the letters JESUS SAVES. On the back of the shirt the message continued AT THE ELLAY NATIONAL BANK.

Mattie, already riled over the ghost issue, was incensed at having her domicile invaded by this stranger. Her red face matched the volume of her voice as she interrupted his chatter. "Just one minute, young man. What do you think you're doing here? If you need anything in this kitchen, I'm the one you should ask. And if you're the caterer for the movie people, you're not cooking in this kitchen. That's for sure."

"A thousand pardons! I did not realize that I was talking to the chatelaine of the castle! Forgive me! I had been given the impression that I was to have use of the kitchen for storing food and preparing meals."

"I'm not the "shatty" or whatever you call it, but as housekeeper and cook, I have a few rights in this area. We'll need to speak to Don Diego about the arrangements for feeding this movie crew. He's the one with the final authority."

"And when does he hold court? Do I need an appointment? I promise to respect all the rules and stay out of your way."

"I think you'd better let me talk to him first. And that T-shirt will not make a very good impression. Don Diego is a very serious and formal gentleman."

Mickey's face fell, and although he seemed humbled under Mattie's severe words, he quickly recovered his aplomb and made a surprising gesture of cooperation. "We can solve that problem with no sweat," he said, and standing with feet apart and throwing his arms across with a theatrical flourish, he peeled the shirt off over his head, turned it around, and put it back on wrong side out. "There," he grinned. "I'm no longer tacky, just scuzzy." But he had moved with the confidence of a magician doing a transformation before his audience, conscious of giving the women a look at his firm torso and muscled arms.

Mattie grunted in disgust and left the room.

Mickey noticed the smile of amusement on Heather's face and, deciding to capitalize on the favorable impression he felt he was making, continued, "While we're reserving space and jurisdiction around here, I'd like to take this opportunity of asking you, Fair Lady, for the first dance at the

Wrap party."

"What's the Wrap party?"

"When the shooting is finished and the film is all in the can, we plan to celebrate. I heard the director say that a week here at most will do it, so before we split, we party. A good idea, don't you think?"

"That sounds like fun. What kind of dancing will it be?" Heather leaned forward showing her interest. Lola picked up the cat, put it on her lap, and settled back to hear more about the party plan.

They were interrupted as Brian entered the kitchen, leading Betty Bergen in to be introduced to the breakfasters.

Betty was dressed in a blue western-style dress with fringed yoke and a silver concho belt around her ample waist that was repeated on the band of her western hat. She smiled ingratiatingly and appeared eager to meet the movie people, but seemed to lose interest when she discovered that none of those present were actors. "We have plenty of room at the Lazy-A if you're too crowded here. Just send over your extra people."

Heather and Betty acknowledged that they'd already met, but Betty avoided any mention of Heather's long walk to find the Castle. "Are you settling in with the ghosts okay?" She pushed a strand of her blond hair back into place with a chubby hand, not realizing she'd hit home with her comment.

Heather laughed nervously and before she could manage a reply, Lola offered, "I'm sure it's a friendly presence. I plan to do a meditation reading to determine what it is and how we'll deal with it."

Betty looked surprised but said, "I hope you have better luck than the previous tenants. They finally gave up and moved out."

Brian wanted to dismiss the whole topic as small talk and, smiling at Heather said, "People coming to high altitude for the first time often have hallucinations. She'll get acclimated pretty soon and I'll bet the ghost will go away."

Mickey added, "If it's a male, it'll be pretty hard to drive it away from Heather's room. A smart ghost knows a cute chick when he sees one."

Heather was gratified to be the object of a compliment regarding her appearance, but disturbed at Brian's dismissal of the topic. She read it as a masculine put-down toward a silly female and felt she wanted to be taken more seriously by this handsome man.

Mattie returned to the kitchen, marching in with an imperious gait and announcing, "Mickey is to have the kitchen through lunch, and we both will do the dinners. With me in charge, of course. And during the mornings, I'll be working as Don Diego's secretary, sorting out his paper-work mountain. You'll see a more organized place here from now on."

Chapter X

The dreamer can know no truth,
not even about his dream,
except by awaking out of it.

—GEORGE SANTANYA

The patio of the Adobe Castle was a clearing formed on three sides by the back walls of the house and bordered by the castle wall on the fourth. There was evidence of attempted improvements as a garden: a clump of brown-eyed Susans near the exit from the kitchen, paths bordered by unevenly trimmed grasses, and pots of blue petunias around a fountain basin. The fountain was dry, the broken statue of a cherub in the center recalling a day when his chubby arm may have held a flowing jug and now thrust only a truncated limb toward the concrete benches and the scattered folding chairs under two giant pine trees and one scrawny apple tree.

It was here that the Castle guests were assembling, talking in excited groups about the accommodations, the unloading of equipment, the plans for tomorrow's filming. Linda London, the beautiful blond actress, was holding court in a corner of the garden, surrounded by a talkative throng. Heather's old hero Jack Hilton now looked taller and younger as he sat near Linda in the darkening shadows of the garden. Another man with strident voice, green beret over dark hair, and bushy mustache seemed to be the focus of the group. Heather smiled at the confirmation of her stereotyped idea that he would be the director. It was true. Pierre Du Von was already giving directions for tomorrow's shooting, waving his arms excitedly, and talking about power cables and supplementary lighting.

The most attractive male of the group was not one of the actors, however. It was Brian, who sat at the edge of the gathering, his foot propped on a folding chair. His broad shoulders made a pleasing angle under a lean and clean-shaven jawline. He looked across the patio at Heather who sat with Lola LaFey on a teetery wooden bench near the kitchen door, holding Malkin and watching

Chippercat who was stalking around them giving throaty growls.

Catching Heather's eye, Brian smiled and rose
to cross the patio to talk with her, but before he
could come away from the group, Pierre Du Von
stopped him, pulled up a chair, and motioning
Brian back to his place, engaged him in what
appeared to be a serious consultation.

Chippercat continued his growling. It wasn't
clear whether Chipper was threatening the tabby
cat with warnings regarding the territory or
merely expressing jealousy of the attention being
given the new comer. He finally waved his big
blue tail in a sideways jerk, went off to the other
side of the patio, and leaped up onto the low wall
where he paraded along the top like a sentinel.
Malkin, relaxed at his departure, began to snuggle
down and purr with contentment.

Heather was waiting for Brian to finish his
deep conversation with the director so he could
talk with her, when Don Diego appeared. He
asked for everyone's attention as if he were opening a convention, his ram-rod posture and bushy
eyebrows creating an imposing presence.

"Welcome to the Adobe Castle! I trust you
found your rooms to be satisfactory. We want to
make your stay pleasant as well as productive. I
have one caution for the people who go running

or walking for exercise. Although I anticipate no trouble, we do have reports of bears in the area. They are usually ready to run away at the sight of people, but it would be wise to venture out only in groups or pairs and to use the upper trail to the road instead of the trail behind the castle."

Laughter and buzzing conversation resumed, and Lola discussed with Heather the question of whether Malkin could detect the presence of bears as well as of ghosts. Lola declared that she was too tired to climb the tower stairs, but advised Heather to take Malkin to the tower room herself and check the cat's reaction. She rose to leave and Heather decided to follow, still carrying Malkin and doubting that the cat would consent to a separation from her mistress. When Lola and Heather parted at the door to Lola's room, Malkin was still riding contentedly in Heather's arms, so Heather carried her on toward the tower stairs.

The lower and upper ends of the stairway were dark, the main light fixture being at the landing where the first flight of stairs ended. Heather caught her breath suddenly as a dark shape sped along the wall past her feet. She breathed easily again when she realized it was only Chippercat. He was not about to let Heather take the visiting cat into the tower without his approval. But when they entered the room, he leaped onto the foot of the bed and strolled around on it, claiming his territory without worrying about Malkin or making any surly noises. Heather put Malkin down on a big easy chair, but Malkin insisted on exploring the room, investigating every corner and sniffing into each cranny as if to acquaint herself with this new area. Was she noticing anything supernatural? And if so, how would she indicate that feeling? Heather had neglected to question Lola on just how this psychically sensitive cat was supposed to perform in the presence of spirits.

When she was finally settled in bed, with Chipper cat curled up at the foot, Malkin was still prowling about the room. There was the comforting idea that any further noises would be the cat and nothing more. She soon slept, her last thoughts mingling the face of the handsome Brian with that of the mysterious soldier in the old fashioned uniform.

But she slept restlessly, the soldier coming and going in her dreams. Finally he seemed to be in the room, moving closer and actually bending over her as she slept.

She sensed the odor of horses, leather, and damp wool. He reached out a hand and touched her cheek.

At his touch she awoke and sat bolt upright, her heart beating wildly. The room was empty. In the soft moonlight shining through the window, she could see Chippercat still curled up and sleeping soundly at the foot of the bed.

But Malkin stood on the floor looking like a Halloween cat with humped back and double-sized tail. The cat's head turned slowly as she seemed to watch an invisible presence moving toward the door.

Then Heather heard each step on the stairs emit a creaking noise as if someone were descending the wooden staircase outside the room.

Chapter XI

*For an actress to be a success she must
have the face of Venus, the brains of Minerva,
the grace of Terpsichore, the memory of
Macaulay, the figure of Juno, and the
hide of a rhinoceros.*

—ETHYL BARRYMORE

Heather sat on a grassy bank across the open meadow before the Castle. At her back was the panoramic spread of the Valley backed by the snow tipped Sangre de Cristo Mountains.

But the scene before her in the courtyard was more interesting. The meadow was swarming with people, equipment, and vehicles as the film makers prepared the movie set. Platforms, cables, and cameras were placed and replaced. Performers, technicians, and grips went in and out of vans and trailers. And dominating the scene were two overseers, Pierre Du Von, who seemed to be everywhere at once, urging haste as he gesticulated, and Don Diego, who strode among the clutter looking like a bewildered plantation overseer whose workers had gone berserk.

Heather was far enough away to enjoy watching the activity without feeling that she would be in the way. Her unnerving experience of the previous night had kept her from sleeping until almost dawn, and when daylight began to show at the windows and her eyes began to close, she was wakened by the stir in the courtyard and decided to go in search of Lola to tell her about the ghostly encounter and to describe Malkin's reaction.

But Lola was already busy in the costume or makeup trailers, and Heather decided to do a short run and return by the courtyard to watch the film preparations from a distance.

The sun was warming the grassy slope where she sat. The trees behind her were unmoving in the still air, and nearby a bee was poised over a tiny flower that looked like a miniature orchid in the grass. Chippercat sneaked along through the grass, sometimes crouching like his feral ancestors in a jungle, and sometimes sniffing or biting on an interesting bit of greenery. Although only mid-morning, the day seemed to have an afternoon somnolence at odds with the activity near the Castle, and a drowsiness which invited her to lie full length as she watched, finally overtook her and she dozed.

Brian was irritated. The setting up was taking longer than it should, Pierre expected him to help prep the set, and because the horses had arrived, Pierre wanted to do the letter scene first. The scene involved having the heroine run toward the mounted soldier to hand him a last-minute warning before he galloped away.

Linda London stood waiting and complaining about the absence of Dorothy, the stunt woman who did most of Linda's outdoor and distance scenes. The trial takes and closeups with the dolly camera were still not finished, but Pierre wanted to get the horse scene completed before the light changed in the meadow. He could see cumulus puffs forming on the horizon and dreaded the retakes which would irritate the main cameraman who abhorred the changing light of a mottled sun-and-shadow setting.

Meanwhile Jack Hilton, who did his own stunts and riding, seemed to enjoy the liveliness of the little brown mare furnished by the Lazy-A stables. He trotted her back and forth at the top of the rise behind the Castle waiting for the scene to be called. His canteen bumping up and down made the mare more skittish than usual and he had twice ridden toward Pierre with the suggestion to move ahead to the next scene. Brian tried to advance the same idea, but Pierre was adamant, and Brian, trying another possibility, called out to Linda, "Could you run up the slope yourself, instead of waiting for Dorothy?"

She turned an icy stare toward him. "I'm paid to act, not to scramble over rocks and logs. I'll be waiting in the green-room van till you're ready for my next take." And with that she strode away, her long blue dress swirling about her booted ankles and her blonde hair bouncing in carefully coiffed waves on her back.

Brian had been aware of Heather's observing them from the distant slope, and as he walked back to inform the cameraman of the hold, he approached Pierre with a new idea. "Can you wait a few more minutes? I may be able to get a stand-in for our stunt gal."

He hiked across the meadow toward the slope as quickly as his sore ankle would allow, and climbing toward Heather, was struck by the idyllic scene before him. In the sparse grass blossomed the flower that looked like a tiny orchid, its delicate beauty matched by the sleeping woman nearby. Her head rested on her arm, her lips were partly open, and her long dark lashes complimented her fair face. He leaned down to examine the flower first with the crazy notion of perhaps picking it to present to her with a compliment before making his request. But as he drew near, a dark form emerged from behind a tree, and a dark hand was thrust palm outward almost in his face. He looked up to see the glowering face of Sam Redfox and to hear his deep voice utter, "Stop! Protected."

Brian wasn't sure at first if the reference was to the sleeping lady or to the blossom, until Sam continued, "Ladyslipper orchid. *Calypso bulbosa montanum*. Rare and not to pick."

Brian muttered an embarrassed and hesitant reply of agreement, startled at the encounter and taken aback by the erudite nomenclature coming from the Indian whom he had considered illiterate.

At the same time Heather awoke, surprised to see two men standing over her. As she sat up she heard Brian saying, "We need your help. Would you like to be in the movies?"

Chapter XII

The pain others give passes away in their later kindness, but that of our own blunders, especially when they hurt our vanity, never passes away.

—WILLIAM BUTLER YEATS

Heather sat on a stool in the green-room trailer while Lola pinned up her hair and arranged the long blond wig to conceal any dark strands of her own hair. The blue dress had been almost a perfect fit, requiring only a few tucks at the waist, but the boots pinched her feet, even with the lacings as loose as possible.

When she agreed at Brian's request to be a stand-in for the stunt actress, she hadn't realized how complicated the preparation would be. Brian had said she would probably be on screen for thirty seconds, filmed from the back as she ran up the slope behind the Castle. But first she had to fill out several forms, sign her name on liability releases and insurance forms, and because she was performing as more than an extra, one of the assistant directors insisted that she be a member of the Film Makers Union. She tried to say she'd help as an unpaid volunteer, but regulations would not allow anything so simple. And enrollment in the FMU required a membership payment before her signature could be accepted. Brian had tried to reason with the assistant director, but finally conceded, taking out his own checkbook and writing a voucher for the required amount.

Even though her face would not show in the film, two makeup people fussed and daubed at it, trying her under different lights that made her eyes hurt.

Then came the walk-through. She stood with her back to the camera, accepted a folded missive from a uniformed actor, and went up the slope toward Jack Hilton, holding up the long dress with her left hand and stepping daintily over low rocks and two fallen logs. On the first take she felt as if she were dreaming. How could she, Heather McMarley Nobody, really be taking part

in a film with Jack Hilton? Jack Hilton, the movie
star cowboy, the one she had watched so many
times from the balcony of the Center Movie
House at home in Illinois. She was grateful that
her face would not show in the film. Her facial
expression was probably one of awe-struck igno-
rance, if not of absolute stupidity.

The awe-struck attitude changed to a determined demeanor as she was made to repeat the
same walk again and again while technicians
called out light-meter readings and cameramen
made endless adjustments.

Finally the real action began and she was
told to run. This was to be the final take. She
had cleared the rocks and the two logs success-
fully when she suddenly tripped on the hem of
the long dress and fell sprawling face down
against the dirt, the letter still clutched in her
hand. She felt the waist seam of the dress give
way, the wig shift on her head, and was aware
of a sharp pain in her arm as she fell, but the
real pain was that of acute embarrassment.
Hearing cries of "Get up, keep going!" she stum-
bled upright and continued up the slope. But to
her disgust she actually tripped twice more
before she reached the mounted cowboy and
handed him the letter. As he took it from her,
the horse reared, and only the quick guidance

of the rider kept the hooves from coming down upon her.

Her chagrin at her own clumsiness was not lessened by the cheers of approval she heard from the crew and the matter-of-fact directive from Pierre for a retake. The dress was pinned, her arm swabbed with antiseptic, and she started again, determined this time to perform perfectly.

But as she neared the logs she was aware of a darkening shadow. The clouds had come across the sun, spoiling the take and causing the main cameraman to spit profanities.

There were three more attempts ordered as the scene was shot with different exposures, two of them being canceled by rapid light changes as the sun went under and came out of the clouds.

Red-faced and breathing heavily, Heather headed back toward the green-room trailer. Linda London, who had watched the entire scene, approached her, her identical blue dress intact and neat, a contrast to Heather's disheveled and dirty one. "Good job," Linda said, holding out her hand to shake Heather's. But her smile was one of smug superiority and the tone of the greeting conveyed an arrogant sarcasm that was obvious to Heather.

Then she saw Brian coming toward her. His face seemed to reflect the embarrassed disappointment on her own, and unable to face his polite thanks, or endure his commiserations, she hurried inside and closed the door before he could reach her.

Chapter XIII

*A difference of taste in jokes is a
great strain on the affections.*

—GEORGE ELIOT

The day's filming accomplished, the crew
were stashing their gear, winding cables, and cov-
ering equipment to be left ready for the next day.
Tex Bergen, Betty's husband, was coaxing the
brown mare into a horse trailer to return to the
Lazy-A stables. Tex really looked more like a fake
cowboy than a ranch foreman. He was medium
height, but his lean build made him appear taller,
and his pale mustache, bleached jeans and faded
shirt gave him a weathered and tentative appearance as if he had stood many years in the wind
and sun and may yet blow away in the next
strong gust. Only his vivid blue eyes and firm jaw

seemed substantial enough to establish him as a definite presence. Even his voice sounded cracked and hesitant as he called to his wife. "Betty, give me a hand with Brownie. The mare's your horse."

Betty was not yet in sight and Heather approached, offering to hold Brownie's halter in the front of the trailer while Tex closed the door.

Tex had been an engrossed spectator. "This movie business sure is interesting. I never knew about all this makeup and fake stuff. That Hilton fellow is just a short guy—has to stand on a chair to be taller than the gal he talks to. I'm surprised he rides his own horse. I'd like to see how the fist-fight scene will get done. I'll bet it's all fake too. I've heard they use stand-ins and furniture that falls apart when you touch it."

He secured the trailer door and turned to thank Heather when he saw that Jack Hilton himself was approaching leading another horse in. His expression showed he had heard Tex's final comments. "Stick around, Podner. You just may get to see one of them fake fights." Tex was too flustered to reply and couldn't determine if Jack's use of cowboy slang was a continuation of his stage dialect or if the actor was actually making fun of Tex's accent.

Before he could frame an appropriate reply, the light near the castle entry went off and someone yelled, "Power out!"

In daylight the lack of electricity would be only a minor inconvenience, but Pierre, concerned about the next day's filming, ran to find Don Diego and determine the cause of the power outage. He passed Betty Bergen, who also seemed in a hurry, eager to leave the Castle and anxious about whether the Lazy-A was also without power. Heather hurried to her tower, hoping for a shower before the water pressure dropped.

The confusion for some of the Castle guests was minimized because Mattie had already cooked the supper, but most of the film crew decided to depart for the lights and entertainment of Santa Fe. It was determined that two blown fuses had caused the power loss, and Brian joined the Santa Fe group in order to purchase replacements. Don Diego invited Pierre and Lola to join him and Heather in the formal dining room for a candlelight supper, and when they were assembled they were a group of five, because they found that Mickey had joined them, his T-shirt changed for a white shirt and plaid jacket. Although she would have preferred Brian as an escort, Mickey gallantly took Heather's arm and led her into the dining room.

Lola seemed distracted and uneasy because Malkin had disappeared. Supper was delayed while everyone searched the yard and ground floor for the cat. When they gave up the unsuccessful search and assembled at the table, the atmosphere was one of gloom. Chippercat took his place atop the high cabinet, his shadow from the light of the candle looming huge on the wall behind him.

Attempting to cheer the diners, Pierre offered pleasantries, beginning with compliments to Heather for her plucky performance of the afternoon and expressing hope that her injuries were minor.

"The main injury was only to my pride," Heather replied. "And I'm sorry I caused so much delay for the filming."

"Repeated takes are to be expected in this business, and the delay for signing you on was not your fault. You really saved the day because we could not have continued otherwise." Pierre's gracious comments helped somewhat, and Heather was about to ask more about the filming when Lola brought the conversation back to Malkin.

"We didn't have time to finish our conversation in the green room trailer, Heather. Tell me more about what Malkin did last night."

As Heather repeated the story of the ghostly encounter, Don Diego began to glower. He finally stiffened in his chair and laying down his fork, said, "Your imagination is overactive. I do not believe there is anything supernatural in the tower, neither in the entire castle. You had a vivid dream and your voice frightened the cat."

Heather began to protest that she had not spoken aloud, when Mickey broke in with a laugh. "I think there really are ghosts in this place. That would explain why our filming was jinxed, why the power went off, and why the cat disappeared. The cat was undoubtedly spirited away. Spirited away, get it?"

But his facetious comment was lost on Lola, who sat fingering her moon pendant as she stared into the candle flames. "I'd like to sit in the tower room for awhile tonight, if you don't mind. I can sometimes detect a supernatural presence, and as a medium, I may be able to bring out some information."

"Of course," Don Diego put in angrily. "We shall join you and help you invite these spirits. We shall be the witnesses."

Mickey seemed delighted. "Do we need to wait till midnight? Will you use an Ouija board?"

"Neither midnight nor Ouija boards are necessary. I would like to sit in a comfortable chair at a small table. Let's eat our dessert, and after coffee, we'll go up."

Mattie clumped in with the dessert just as Lola spoke, and her audible grunt of disgust brought Don Diego's brows down in a severe frown, but the atmosphere softened as the diners enjoyed the raspberry natillas, a creamy concoction that drew compliments and restored everyone's composure. Mickey seemed especially delighted, and finishing his dessert before anyone else, left to get a card table for the tower room.

Don Diego ordered flashlights for each guest to carry as they left the dining room. Pierre, protesting fatigue, excused himself from the proposed séance, but the other four climbed the tower stairs, their lights stabbing the darkness with beams that created fitful shadows as they went up.

Mickey had already placed the card table in the center of the tower room, and as Don Diego seated himself across from him, the two exchanged looks of skeptical amusement. Heather faced Lola who sat in a large Victorian armchair wearing an expression of serious contemplation. The filmy, multilayered lavender collar of her dress made a delicate and diaphanous frame for her face, and the light from a small candle in the center of the table gave an ethereal look to her eyes.

Until silenced by Lola, Mickey kept laughing and moving his flashlight beam about the room teasing Chippercat who was following and jumping at the beam of light.

Ultimately stillness prevailed and the room was quiet enough to reveal the ticking of Heather's windup travel clock and the rustling of papers as Chipper rummaged in a wastebasket.

Mickey broke the silence with his suggeston. "Shouldn't we be touching hands on the table? Isn't it supposed to rock to answer the questions we ask?"

Lola seemed absorbed enough in her concentration to ignore the questions, but Mickey put his hand on Heather's and gave it a pressure that was more than a spiritual touch.

Minutes passed. Heather was beginning to feel drowsy, but she suddenly became aware of an odor, the same aroma she had detected in the presence of the ghostly visitor. She looked up at the others, wondering if they had noticed it also.

Then they became aware of a low knocking sound, not from the table, but from inside the large armoire. It was not the cat; they could see Chipper who was now sitting quietly atop the bedside table. As the sound was repeated, he jumped down and ran toward the armoire, and at the same time, the light in the closet came on.

"The power is restored," Don Diego muttered. "Brian must have replaced the fuses."

But the spell was broken. They could hear distant noises of the crew returning from town, and in the light from the closet they could see Chipper jumping at something near Mickey's foot.

Lola stood up abruptly and extinguished the candle. "I see we have a joker here," she said. "We'll have to continue the spirit search another time." And she opened the armoire door to reveal a shoe fastened to a string, the other end of which was tied to the leg of Mickey's chair. His pressure on the string had caused the shoe to bump the armoire door.

Discovered in his trickery, Mickey laughed and explained, "If it hadn't been for that cat, I'd have had you."

Don Diego chuckled in triumph. "You see how all strange noises have a logical explanation." He pushed back his chair and followed Mickey out of the room. Heather turned on the light near the door and prepared to follow Lola down the stairs. First she went over to the closet to turn that light off. As she reached for the switch, the light went off by itself. "Did you see that?" she asked Lola.

"There really are strange forces here," Lola answered. "But we will investigate them in more favorable circumstances." She picked up the cat and started down the staircase.

Chapter XIV

Every calamity is a spur and valuable hint.

—RALPH WALDO EMERSON

The sound of music came from the big kitchen as Lola and Heather reached the bottom of the stairs. Investigating, they found several of the film crew extending their Santa Fe partying to the accompaniment of a little boom-box tape player. Jack Hilton and Linda London were dancing a polka together, circling the big table where several spectators urged them on by clapping and cheering.

Seeing Heather in the doorway, Mickey grabbed her hand and swung her into the polka. She had no chance to resist nor any breath left during the dance to express her disappointment at Mickey's deception, and she knew that he had no awareness that his joke had not been as entertaining as he had intended.

Brian entered from outside and found a seat near the door just as the polka ended, and as Jack released Linda, she sank laughing onto Brian's lap. She threw her arms around his neck and said, "Our hero! The man who restored the power."

Brian, at first surprised and embarrassed, then pleased, accepted the accolade by smiling and encircling Linda with his arms. She did not offer to move, and as the music began again, Jack approached Heather and bowing first, extended his hand to dance with her. Mickey pulled another young woman from among the spectators, some of whom were rising to join the dancing.

Heather's thrill at dancing with her old film star hero was cut short by the entrance of Mattie. She stood in the doorway wearing her bathrobe, the pink hair roller atop her head, and an annoyed expression on her face. "How long will this be going on? I'm trying to get some sleep and I was told that you movie people wanted an early breakfast."

The music suddenly ceased and attention was focused on the other door where Don Diego had entered. He said nothing, but his presence, like an angry father surprising the children at an unauthorized party, effectively ended the impromptu festivity. The party guests slowly headed back to their rooms. Heather noticed that Linda, evidently pleased with her place on Brian's knee, was one of the last to leave. She leaned back and whispered in Brian's ear as she rose.

Mickey, unabashed, ended the scene with another laugh. "That was O.K. for a warmup, but we want a full mariachi band for the wrap party." He directed his order at Don Diego, positive that the stern host had no thoughts other than catering to his guests.

Instead of hearing an answer Mickey heard something else. "What was that? Listen! Bears in the yard?" And grabbing a big flashlight from the table, he ran out the door to the rear of the castle.

Don Diego and Brian followed and Heather heard Mickey shout again. "Bandits! Come look."

In the beam of his flashlight Heather saw a large raccoon and three little ones. Before they scuttled away, they looked inquiringly into the light. Their faces with the dark band across the eyes like little masks did indeed give them the look of bandits. They had tipped over a large trash can and were rummaging the contents when the noise brought the interruption in their late-night investigations.

"The trash can needs to be secured." Don Diego, addressing Mickey, continued, "Por favor assist me in lifting this can to a safer place inside the wall."

When the others had disappeared inside, Heather and Brian stood alone in the darkness. She looked up to see the small patch of sky above them blazing with hundreds of stars. Dazzlingly spectacular in their vivid sparkling against the black sky, they gave the impression of hanging almost within reach above the trees.

Brian followed her gaze. "Have you ever seen such a sky? There are so many stars I can't make out any constellation patterns. Where is the Big Dipper?"

"It must be behind the trees. And there's no moon, so the stars seem brighter. What's that little blob of cloud?"

"Where?" And in order to follow her line of sight, he moved closer to stand behind her, putting his hand on her shoulder. "It must be that comet. Comet Tofu, or something. We heard about it on the van radio. They said it's now visible to the naked eye."

"What luck. It shows in the one patch of sky we can see."

Heather was still in awe at the clarity of the Southwestern skies.

"Shouldn't we make a wish? Or is that just for seeing falling stars? I'll bet Lola will see it as an omen and warn us about some terrible thing about to happen. Did she scare away your ghost?"

"She can't detect anything of the paranormal as long as there are jokers around." And Heather told him about the aborted séance in the tower room.

"You're barking up the wrong tree. I've discovered something which I'll ask you to keep quiet about. I found that the power outage was not caused by blown fuses. Someone had actually removed the fuses."

"Who would want to do that? And why? Are you suggesting that someone is trying to sabotage the filming?"

"I'm going to try to find out. And if it's the same person who's hanging around your tower room, I'd like to catch him before his next move."

Heather shivered with the cold and with the annoyance she felt. "You'll never accept the fact that the tower room problem is not a living person. It's cold out here. I'm going inside."

But before she could leave, Brian pulled her toward him. "Stay a little longer. Here's my jacket." And he put it around her shoulders. "Let me check your door tonight. I want to get to the bottom of this. I want to clear up your ideas on this problem. Let's talk. Walk over to the overlook with me. We can see more of the sky from there."

"I don't think we're communicating. If you're trying to clear up my thinking, you're going about it in the wrong way."

"Let me explain," he protested.

"I don't like being told I'm imagining things, and I certainly don't need your protection in my room." She started to walk away.

"Wait," he called after her. But she ran ahead before he could offer any further words on the subject.

Chapter XV

I have no objections to churches so long as they do not interfere with God's work.

—Brooks Atkinson

Heather slept deep and peacefully, exhausted by the exertions and excitement of the day. It would be impossible to determine whether any ghosts stayed away in scorn of the sham séance, or that they came but were unable to pierce the heavy slumber which held her.

When she awoke she needed several minutes to remember where she was and to recall the previous day's events. Seeing her dusty shoes brought back the scene of her film debut with her stumbling run and embarrassing fall. Then she saw Brian's brown leather jacket on a chair. In her fit of pique she had marched off still wearing it. She decided to return it to the kitchen where the impromptu party had taken place.

Dressed to run, she grabbed the jacket and started down the stairs but was stopped by a strange sight. In the alcove at the turning of the last flight of stairs was Brian, asleep on an Indian blanket. He had curled up, fully dressed, in order to fit the narrow alcove, his head at an awkward angle and his feet protruding into the hallway.

The strong handsome face and his awkward position locked in sleep gave him a vulnerable look of boyish innocence and evoked at first a feeling of pity for his sincerity. He really believed a prowler might come up the stairs and had posted himself as a sentinel to protect her.

Then she felt with disgust her inability to convince him of the truth of her experiences in the tower room. She gathered up her scorn along with the jacket and threw it over him. "Thanks for the loan of the jacket. And thanks for guarding the stairway. You must have kept all the monsters away!"

He sat up, grabbing at conscious awareness with mumbled comments, shocked to see Heather standing there, chagrined that he had not awakened before she came, and engulfed by the ill humor he felt at her scorn. She ran down the stairs before he could frame a coherent, "You're welcome, I'm sure."

Heather ran on the driveway toward the road remembering Don Diego's warning about bears. She wondered if a bear, or perhaps a coyote, had gotten the cat. Poor Malkin was perhaps lying somewhere in these woods this morning, a half-eaten and mangled little corpse. As she picked up her pace, her thoughts flew faster also. Shunning the thought of feline disaster, she remembered she was supposed to be composing a murder mystery. Running usually brought her a heightened creativity, the words and phrases that she could later put on paper to arrange for best effect. But her mind was locked on the strange and interesting guests of the Adobe Castle, the disturbing presence of the attractive Brian, and the mysterious atmosphere of her tower room.

She had gained the main road and started along it up a steeper rise when she was met by a flatbed wagon pulled by two horses and filled with a group of singing people. Betty and her husband were taking their Lazy-A Dude Ranch guests for a morning outing. As Tex stopped the horses, the song "I've Been Working on the Railroad" ended and Heather was invited to jump on. "Join us. We're going to church!"

Church? Then she realized this was Sunday. "What church? I'm not dressed for church."

"Little Woodsy Church. Non-denominational. We're not wearing Sunday clothes either, and we'll be the entire congregation, so come on and make it a bigger group." Tex seemed proud that he had made the invitation, and Betty beamed at her from under her big Stetson. The friendly guests shoved into a tighter line on their straw bale seats, and Heather stepped up at the rear of the wagon.

She found herself seated between a middle-aged lady wearing dark glasses and cowboy hat, and an elderly mustachioed gentleman wearing a green baseball cap. They proved to be father and daughter, and their principal interaction was the old man's grumbling remarks, followed by his daughter's placating responses.

He began with, "Too many people on this wagon. Can't make any speed. Horses ain't really fit for pulling. These are riding ponies. Darned funny these people couldn't rig up a decent wagon. Sitting on these bales is killing my back."

"It won't be for long, Dad," his daughter replied. "They say the church is just up the way."

"I don't know why we're going to church, anyway. We never go at home. You say it's an excuse now for a wagon ride, but I think it's an excuse to squeeze more money out of us. Mark my words, there'll be a collection plate. Already paid too much for this danged dude-ranch week. Supposed to help my blood pressure, but bringing me to high altitude and going through all these shenanigans won't do it a bit of good, I'll tell you right now."

"But Dad, it's really a beautiful forest, and we're having such good meals. You liked the big breakfast with the apple pancakes, didn't you? And this little outing will give us some fresh air. You don't need to put anything in the collection plate."

She was interrupted by the stopping of the wagon and Tex's announcement, "All out! Time to get our morning exercise and rest the horses a bit. This is our only steep hill, but it's pretty short. Pick you up at the top."

Heather didn't wait to hear the old man's grumbling reaction. She jumped down quickly, deciding she would definitely sit in a different seat for the next part of the trip.

As the wagon pulled ahead, Betty, on the bench next to Tex, called out, "How are the ghosts at the castle? Did anyone film them for the movie?" Her laughter and the questions aroused immediate interest in the group as they walked up the hill. Their questions flew, and Heather tried to parry them with laughter and non-committal replies.

But the new topic furnished fresh grist for the old man's grumble mill. "Ghosts? Hotels will try anything to entertain the guests. We're all suckers, that's what we are. Lazy-A gets customers by advertising True Southwestern Atmosphere, and then adding chili powder to every thing they cook. 'Red or green?' they keep asking. Your castle hotel has probably rigged up some recorded noises so they can ask, 'Haunted or not haunted?' when you book a room. And they probably charge double for the haunted ones."

Heather ran on ahead rather than explain her vacation situation. At the top of the hill she could see a turning in the road and the edge of a small white building, so she continued on to arrive at the church, which proved to be a miniature replica of a Midwestern frame church with pointed windows and a tiny bell-tower box atop a peaked roof. But the cross atop the tower was missing, the front porch was rather sagging, and even the sign in front, NON DENOM, had missing letters with the rest of the label faded to illegibility.

A pickup truck was the only vehicle in the yard, and from the open front door came the sound of guitar music and someone singing,

"Come to the church in the wildwood. Come to the church in the vale." Looking in, she saw two women standing at the altar, the guitar player who was a fluffy haired brunette in long skirt and high heels, and a tall woman with straight brown hair wearing a dark robe.

Heather had not been a regular church goer, but she remembered being taken by her parents on Easter and Christmas, always wearing a lacy dress, shiny Mary Jane shoes, a bonnet and white gloves. And though this visit to a miniature chapel was more of a tourist jaunt than a serious Sunday observance, she recoiled at the thought of entering the building wearing shorts and running shoes. She was spared the decision when she saw that the chuch was too small to accommodate the entire group. Three tiny pews on either side of the center aisle had room for only three people each, forcing the rest of the congregation to stand at the back or on the porch outside. Heather managed to be one of the porch standees, and for a better view she went around to an open side window where she could see as well as hear the service.

The woman in the robe was evidently a lay reader, and the sermon was one prepared for wholesale distribution to mission parishes lacking a regular priest or rector. The robed woman read in an earnest but uninflected tone, and the content was so devoid of scriptural references it could have been an address by a women's club president to her state convention. It was truly ecumenical, thought Heather, but equally uninspiring.

At the conclusion the fluffy haired guitarist struck up the "Battle Hymn of the Republic," a hymn chosen to be non-sectarian yet familiar enough to be sung without a hymnbook. The guitarist's smile and enthusiastic singing almost made up for the lack of inspiration in the sermon. The congregation responded with hearty voices and left the little church with the smug satisfaction that they had performed their Sabbath obligation.

Boarding the wagon before the others, Heather sat toward the front, deciding it would be better to hear Betty's joking about the ghosts than to sit between the curmudgeon and his daughter. The group were almost all on board when they realized they were waiting for the curmudgeon himself. He stood in the doorway engaged in a serious conversation with the robed woman.

The wagonload waited silently, able to hear only the daughter's worried, "Oh, dear, I wonder what he's lecturing her on now. This is so embarrassing."

When he finally boarded and the wagon began to move away, he made a statement that entertained everyone and gained general approval: "She's going to send out a priest to exorcise the demons of your castle. I challenged her to do something to show that the church was good for something besides passing the collection plate and subjecting us to these canned sermons."

Chapter XVI

Violence is essentially wordless, and it can begin only where thought and rational communication have broken down.

—Thomas Merton

The evening was descending with an unsettled atmosphere. The wind, which had earlier gusted to dangerous speed and caused Pierre to call a halt to the filming, had ceased, leaving an uncertain and ominous stillness. Most of the clouds were scattered and light, but over the mountain to the west hung a darker mass which seemed foreboding. The air felt like the proverbial calm before the storm, but the storm failed to materialize. Even though it was still daytime, a nightowl gave a distant lonely cry.

Heather and Lola sat on the patio bench discussing the strange aura of uncertainty that seemed to hover around the Castle. Chippercat was parading nervously atop the patio wall, moving his tail in uneven swings.

"He seems affected by the weather too," Heather remarked. "I wonder if he knows where Malkin is."

Lola leaned back with a sigh against the adobe wall and smoothed her long Indian skirt over her knees. "I have the feeling that Malkin will return. I don't know how, but I'm hoping she's not injured. If Chipper is as insensitive to other influences as you mentioned, I doubt if he's aware of anything unusual. He probably just heard that owl but doesn't know how to find it."

"Do you feel that we will solve the mystery of the tower room disturbances?" Heather asked.

Lola fingered her moon pendant and spoke more slowly. "I don't feel able until Malkin returns, to go to the tower room to concentrate on that problem. But I do have a message for you now." She got up and pulled a folding chair toward the bench. Sitting on it so she could face Heather, she took Heather's left hand in her right and turned it palm up.

"Are you going to read my palm?"

"Only in a general way. The message I have for you comes as a mental picture, but contact with your hand can help focus my concentration."

Heather looked at the broad hand that held her own. Lola wore two large silver rings with turquiose sets. She looked down at Heather's smaller hand with the slim tapering fingers.

"I see you are going to have a visitor quite soon."

"Is it someone I know?" Heather felt goosebumps rise on her arms.

"I think so. But I sense a negative aura here. You will not be pleased with this visitor. But you are not in any danger."

"Can you see farther into the future? Will I succeed in graduate school?" Her hand felt cold and she shifted uneasily on the bench.

"I cannot tell beyond the immediate future. But I feel you may have an affair of the heart. I see a diamond solitaire ring. But the ring is in the sky, not on your finger. Am I right in assuming there is someone special in your thoughts?"

Heather felt her face redden. "I am attracted to someone. But I have mixed feelings."

Lola smiled, her gap-toothed grin narrowed her eyes with merry amusement. "Your feelings will become more clear. The ring will be important."

She leaned forward and seemed about to add more comments when Mickey appeared in the doorway and called, "All-cast meeting! Pierre wants us in the kitchen."

Lola dropped Heather's hand, patted her arm and rose to the summons. "We'll talk another time. This unsettled atmosphere is affecting everyone."

The tower suite seemed warm and peaceful. No strange atmosphere penetrated the room, but Heather was an extra long time falling asleep, her mind full of Lola's predictions. She could not imagine a visitor coming to see her at the Adobe Castle, so she projected the possibility into the future, thinking of distant friends and relatives who could possibly visit. But of all the possibilities, none would be considered unwelcome. How could she take Lola's predictions seriously?

And the diamond ring in the sky. How strange. Did Lola's vision mean that Heather would also see a ring in the sky? Or perhaps this was the distant possibility of an engagement or marriage? She tried to turn her thoughts away from Brian but kept seeing his ingratiating smile.

She felt she had not slept long when a noise awakened her. Chippercat ran to the window and jumping up onto the sill, tried to see what was causing the disturbance. Heather's first thought was that the noise was not of supernatural origin because Chipper had ignored all previous ghostly sounds.

The noise like a muffled scuffling continued, accompanied by angry voices seeming to come from the stairwell. She turned on the light, grabbed her robe and went out into the hall. The scuffling sounds and a bang as if someone were falling against the wall lured her down to the next landing where she looked over the bannister to see a shocking sight.

Brian, the back of his shirt torn, was holding a stranger against the wall. Blood flowed from the dark haired stranger's nose into his mustache as he struggled to free himself. "Let me go, you goon!"

Brian, breathing heavily, was pushing to keep his struggling adversary against the wall. "Explain your business! You don't belong here!"

"I'm a registered guest. Let me explain. What kind of place is this?"

A third voice interrupted. "Gentlemen, please!" It was Don Diego, wearing a black robe and holding a saber.

Heather looked with a shock of recognition at the bleeding man against the wall. "Robbie! Stop! It's my brother. Let him go!"

Chapter XVII

Love is like lightning, swift, electric,
and blinding.

—IVAN ASHROTH

In the settling of the confusion came embarrassed exchanges.

"Robbie, what are you doing here?"

Robbie wiped the blood from his nose with the back of his hand and catching his breath said, "Trying to find out what you're doing here. Gramps thinks you're in a den of iniquity."

"But why did you come all this way? You knew I was on my vacation trip."

Heather's explanation was interrupted by laughter from the hall. Mickey had arrived and now saw a chance to taunt the unfortunate

Brian. "Nice play, Ox!" he said. "You want to impress the princess, so you decide to beat up her brother?"

Brian began to explain. "He wouldn't identify himself. What was he doing prowling around here?"

"Why should I have to identify myself to you? I checked in and was on my way to my room."

"Gentlemen, Gentlemen. There has been a great misunderstanding. Let us close this conversation." Don Diego sheathed his sword and attempted to dismiss the guests. Brian began offering apologies and further explanation, but was cut short by Don Diego. "Señor Minter, there is no need for you to guard the hallways. The Adobe Castle is safe and all our guests are respectable people."

While Heather talked with Robbie and tended to his bloody nose, the other spectators returned to their rooms. Before the brother and sister conversation was over, Mattie appeared and her consternation had to be calmed by an explanation of the preceding contretemps. Finally Mattie led Robbie to his room and Heather returned to hers, to regain repose only after much tossing and mulling.

The arrival of her brother had been surprise enough, but Heather was in bed before further amazement struck her. Lola's prediction had proven true. Here was her visitor and he certainly was not welcome. Three years older than Heather, he had always dominated her grandfather's attention and had been given privileges denied to Heather while mocking her with his one-upmanship in doing so. With his grandfather's indulgence, he had worked only sporadically, refusing to select any career and occupying his life with his sports cars, parties, and the admiring attention of young women that he seemed to attract without any effort.

Even though he had done her a favor in helping to persuade her grandfather to let Heather go off on the New Mexico vacation, she hoped he would not stay long. He had always loved the movies, talked about Hollywood, and believed he belonged in California. Perhaps this was only a stop on his trans-American trip and she could look forward to his early departure.

Loved the movies. She realized that that was the very attraction that could keep him at the Castle. When he discovered that film making was in progress, he would want to stay. Shooting of the final scenes was being done and the film nearly complete. But so was her vacation. She fell asleep with the determination to accomplish more writing on her story outline and to ignore the annoyance of her brother's presence.

The next morning found the two former adversaries, along with Mickey, gathered around the sleek red sports car. Their heads were together under the hood, and while Robbie demonstrated the features of the car, Brian and Mickey listened attentively and poked inquisitively into the engine.

The atmosphere seemed more settled than it had been the previous night, and although the sky was not clear, the evenness of the cloud cover created a stable lighting situation that was pleasing to the cameramen, and the shooting of the final scenes was in progress.

When Heather returned from her morning run she circled to the front of the set to watch Linda and Jack performing a difficult scene. The seated couple repeated the dialogue patiently as Pierre strove for more perfect angles and complained about the background. A group of interested spectators watched intently.

But the most interested person was Robbie. He sat as close to the performers as Pierre's permission would allow and leaned forward with elbows on his knees staring at the beautiful Linda with a fascination that indicated total absorption and absolute admiration. He was smitten. Heather saw that there could be no hope of Robbie's early departure.

Then out of the calm sky with no warning, lightning struck. The discharge was so near and the noise so great that the shock stunned everyone. The transformer on the high pole behind the castle had attracted the electricity from the sky, and the light illuminated the nearby trees with a great flash as the tremendous crash echoed in a resounding reverberation into the canyon.

After the initial shock and grateful realization that no one had been injured came the awareness that the electric power supply had been cut off again.

"Curses! Foiled again," joked Mickey.

Pierre was not amused. He kept removing his beret and slamming it back onto his head as he paced angrily and uttered terrible curses in French.

Brian was the first to offer a positive suggestion."We need a generator. The sound stage at the Santa Fe studio has one. If it's working, I can bring it up on their truck and restore power by this afternoon."

"And I can drive you down in my car," Robbie offered. He was happy to be a part of the filming by helping in the emergency and by having the opportunity to demonstrate the power of his engine. The two men sped off up the forest road in the red car before anyone could make any objections.

Later that afternoon, the portable generator was in operation. It had been set up far enough in the back of the castle grounds so that its noise would not interfere with the filming, but the power output was enough for the lights and camera equipment only. The Castle itself had to return to candles and kerosene lanterns, although Mattie insisted that the refrigerators and water pumps be switched back on as soon as the afternoon scenes were completed.

Chapter XVIII

Delay always breeds danger and to protract a great design is often to ruin it.

—Miguel de Cervantes

That evening Heather determined that neither the worry over an unwelcome brother or the thought of any supernatural manifestations would disturb her rest. As long as she felt no physical contact from spectral sources, she decided she had nothing to fear from visions, aromas, or noises. So firm was her resolution that she was able to ignore the shadowy materialization which she was sure was lurking in the far corner of the room as she undressed, and to shut her ears, with the help of the quilt over her head, to the sound of intermittent tapping near the window. Her resolution kept her immersed in a sleep so sound that she was unaware of the moon, which had shrunk from its last-quarter, half-moon shape and was rising now as a thin letter C, which faded to invisibility as the streaks of dawn brightened into the cobalt sky of day.

But as she floated upward to the surface of wakefulness, she was accompanied by a dream. In it she saw her grandfather's face frowning at her as she unloaded little black boxes, each containing a cat. On waking and smiling at the dream, the black boxes reminded her of the case containing the camera given to her by her grandfather as she was leaving for her Western trip. She realized that her vacation time was dwindling and she had not as yet taken any photos. Maybe today would bring a chance to get some candid shots of the filming. She knew that Robbie would want pictures of the beautiful Linda. And Grandfather would surely be impressed with a picture of the Adobe Castle.

Her last conversation with him showed that he still felt distrustful of her vacation milieu.

"Is that Adobe Castle run by foreigners?" he had asked. "The fellow who answered the phone had a pretty thick accent."

"Don Diego is Spanish. He's very well educated."

"Are they all a bunch of Mexicans? I don't like the idea of your staying with a bunch of foreigners."

"Spanish, not Mexican. His ancestors were people from Spain, and this is New Mexico, a state of the United States, not Mexico."

"Well, it sounds pretty foreign to me. I hope you're keeping your door locked and being careful who you talk to."

The conversation had not reassured him, and Heather ended by saying that her next call would probably be the one from the railway station at home after she arrived there the following week.

Later that morning as she sat across the meadow to watch the continuation of the previous day's filming with her camera ready, she realized she was too far away, and lacked a zoom lens to catch the actors in the proper focus. Robbie had resumed his stunned stare from a close vantage point, but Heather felt embarrassed, for there was her hero Jack Hilton, standing on a low stool in order to appear taller than Linda, who was looking up at him as the cameras recorded a closeup. Seeing the reality behind the filmed romance was like keyhole peeping and quite disillusioning. She decided against trying to take any pictures then.

Puffy cumulus clouds began to dot the sky and slowed the filming. Today's clouds seemed to be rising faster than usual and sunny breaks coming at less frequent intervals. Along with cooler air came a gusty wind. Spectators buttoned up or went for jackets, and finally the sky darkened to release huge wet drops. But mixed with them, to everyone's amazement, were flakes of snow. Huge and wet, they melted as soon as they landed, but the combination of snow and thunder was an exciting anomaly for the visitors, and even though the sudden storm sent the film crew to shut down, Heather decided to put on a rain jacket and walk along the path to take some scenery photos which would indeed prove this to be an exotic place.

As she left the castle environs, the snow was coming thicker and some of it was staying on the ground, making the pathway a solid white walkway. But the wind and increasing snow-rain mixture made walking unpleasant and shrouded the view of the valley. Even from a higher vantage point on the trail the scene was not worth photographing, so she decided to take only one picture, the Adobe Castle, a dark fortification looming in the storm of white. Her hands were wet and cold as she put the camera back under her jacket and turned again toward the castle. In the exposed places of the path she noticed her own footprints, the little triangles of the tread on the soles already being obscured by the falling snow. But at the juncture with another trail she saw another set of footprints fresher than her own outward bound marks. Their tread showed concentric circles and the prints were considerably larger than her own. Someone else must have wanted the brief novelty of a winter walk in August.

When she entered the castle kitchen, she saw that it was dark. The generator had quit and the power had gone off again. Pierre was pacing and muttering his disgust with the weather and the consequent delay. Mattie was standing with arms akimbo looking disgusted at the muddly smudges his feet made on the clean floor.

Mickey was unpacking boxes of food and supplies and equally disgusted because the contents of one carton did not match the label. "Cracker Jacks? I ordered crackers and they gave me Cracker Jacks! What a bunch of bozos. Can't you see us putting Cracker Jacks in the soup and scooping out the little prizes?"

Betty and Tex were taking shelter from the storm and awaiting Pierre's decision about the horses. Should they wait to see if the weather cleared? Pierre ignored them as he paced and grumbled.

Brian entered and Pierre turned to him saying, "Is everything stashed? I'm about ready to move out of here. We can't seem to get these scenes into the can and we're already over budget. If we keep losing power we can't finish anyway."

The only happy creature in the darkening kitchen was Chippercat. He sat hunched on a rug by the fireplace like a contented Buddha, his forepaws curled in, eyes blinking slowly as he enjoyed the warmth of the flames and the satisfaction of being the only cat of the Castle.

Chapter XIX

Sturm und Drang

—F.M. KLINGER

Brian went looking for Robbie. He hoped that Robbie could help determine the cause of the generator failure. Just as he went out of the kitchen Betty and Tex repeated their offer to house the crew if power could not be restored. They decided to leave for the Lazy-A, Pierre repaired to his quarters, and the remainder of the kitchen crowd took solace in friendly conversation over coffee. The wood range was fired up, the kettle bubbled, and the warmth of the room began to evaporate the gloom and to enhance the spirit of camaraderie.

Mickey was the focus of the group as he began expostulating and engaging in dramatic gestures as he spoke. "We're jinxed I tell you. It's an evil force that doesn't want any film making." He lowered his voice as he lengthened the word evil, bent his knees, and swept his arms outward. Laughter encouraged his dramatics.

Mattie was stirring the contents of a large kettle. She seemed to be the only one unamused by Mickey's antics. "It's not a ghost, but I'm beginning to believe there's a hex on this castle. This may be our last group of guests. I'm going to suggest bankruptcy proceedings. We can't seem to get out of debt, and without a clear title, we can't be financed for more money."

Lola pulled her big shawl around her shoulders more tightly and asked, "Do you think Don Diego will sell to the Lazy-A people? They keep offering to help and almost trying to lure the guests to their ranch."

Mattie turned and held her ladle up to emphasize her words. "No way. Don Diego would never consent to giving up his ancestral home."

"But without a clear title, he may have to let those who have prior claim take over."

Everyone looked in surprise at Sam Redfox as he continued, "He may lose the land to those of us who believe they have prior ownership."

Sam Redfox had spoken. And his words had more dramatic effect than all of Mickey's antics. The quiet native American had reminded them that the mountain was originally the sacred hunting area of his people, the ancient people who now had boundaries lined out by the Forest Service and by old Spanish land grants.

Mickey returned the spotlight to himself by commenting, "Don Diego will never get rid of the ghost, anyway. He should just advertise it as an attraction to the hotel."

Jack Hilton pulled his chair closer to join the conversation. "Can't you just call in an exorcist? One of those priests or people who sprinkle incense and do the magic words?"

"Somebody already had that idea, but Don Diego got rid of her this morning." Mickey smiled smugly at having this latest news to impart.

Heather stiffened in her chair. "How do you know?"

"Her? Was it a woman priest?" Jack asked.

"Because I saw the whole thing this morning, and yes, it was a woman. I'll tell you how it happened. I was getting supplies from the van when this car comes up. Don Diego Ramirez was watering the little shrub at the doorway, and here comes a woman wearing a dark dress with a little white collar like a priest's."

Mickey warmed to his tale, and enjoying the attention, raised his voice and began reenacting the scene for his audience.

"She introduces herself and says she's here to purify a room. Don Diego says, *Purify what room? We have no need of a housekeeper.* And she says, *No, I'm a priest. I was sent here because of a request to rid an apartment of a disturbing spirit.* And you should've seen Señor Ramirez. His jaw stood out as far as his eyebrows and he really told her off. *In the first place, we have no disturbing spirits. And in the second place,* he adds, *if I needed a priest I would ask for a real priest. In my church, women are not priests. You have been misinformed and I am sorry to tell you that you have driven all this way to learn that your services are not wanted. Good morning to you, Señora.* And he turns his back and stalks off like this."

Mickey imitated the imperious stride of Don Diego and reveled in the laughter that greeted his performance.

Mattie looked at Heather. "Who asked for the priest?"

Heather turned red but protested truthfully, "Don't look at me."

The buzz of further comments was interrupted by the entrance of Brian and Robbie. In his arms Brian was carrying a disheveled bundle of scraggly fur. It was Malkin. Her wet fur which was missing in patches, clung to her thin body. One eye was swollen shut and the other one stared with fearful distrust. She had obviously fought with an animal larger than herself and had fared the worse in the combat.

With a cry of welcome, Lola swept the pitiful animal into her arms and began ministering to it with comforting greetings. Mattie brought warm water and soft rags to help doctor the victim, and Malkin submitted docilely to the ministrations.

As a counter to the happy return of Lola's pet, the two men had bad news to relate. The generator was ruined. Someone had put sugar into the gas tank, fouling the engine and making it impossible to operate.

The kitchen group grew silent. Heather suddenly remembered the shoe print in the snow. It had been at the end of the path coming from the area of the generator. She unconsciously looked down at everyone's shoes before realizing that there would be no way to look at the soles and match the pattern to a suspected saboteur.

The silence was broken by the sound of laughter and horses' hoofs as a wagon drew up outside. "Come see the bears!" someone shouted. The kitchen door opened as Betty and Tex entered, inviting everyone to join the hayride to the garbage dump to see the bears.

In reply to the objections that it was dark outside, Tex explained this was the time the bears came out of the forest to rummage at the Forest Service landfill in the canyon a few miles down the road. "We have big flashlights we turn on so you can see them from across the canyon. Last week there was a mother and two cubs."

Heather had an urge to look at the soles of Tex or Betty's shoes. By going along on the ride, she would possibly find a chance to see if their shoe soles matched the prints she had seen on the path that led to the generator.

"Let's go!" she cried. "I've never seen bears outside of a zoo. My vacation's almost over and I want to see all the wildlife I can."

Chapter XX

*It is a matter of regret that many low,
mean suspicions turn out to be well founded.*

—EDGAR WATSON HOWE

Several of the movie people decided to go on
the bear-watching expedition, Jack Hilton, Linda,
and Robbie among them. Brian, concerned about
the damage to the generator, decided instead to
find Pierre and tell him the bad news.

The snow had melted, but the evening chill
was sharp, and Tex agreed to wait while the
guests went to get coats and sweaters for the ride.
Betty sat on the driver's bench holding the reins,
her feet on the slanted footrest. Heather, already
carrying her jacket, was the first to board. She
came around to the front of the wagon and

caught her breath sharply as she saw the exposed part of the soles of Betty's boots. They were concentric circles, the print she had seen in the snow at the back of the castle during the storm.

She climbed up onto the seat directly behind Betty and was about to make a conversational comment about walking during the storm when she saw the top of a sack sticking out of the pocket of Betty's sheepskin jacket. Without thinking, she pulled it out and read aloud, "Southern Sugar, Extra Fine Granulated."

"Did you find this out by the generator?"

Betty, alarmed, turned around, grabbed the sack and stuck it deep back into her pocket as she said, "Old lunch sack. Never mind."

But Tex had seen the exchange and heard the accusatory tone of Heather's voice. He grabbed the front of her shirt and pulled her down off the wagon, saying, "What're you sayin' Miss? You better be careful of your words and you better keep your hands to yourself." His voice became deep and threatening and he pulled her close to emphasize his statement.

"What about your own hands? Let me go. I only asked a question. I'm not going on the wagon." She struggled free of his grasp and ran back into the Castle, just as the rest of the passengers were emerging with their coats and heading for the wagon.

In answer to the puzzled queries from the others, Tex explained, "Fraid of bears. Decided not to go." And he made short work of helping them to board the wagon, then clucked to the horses to move away quickly from the courtyard.

In the dark kitchen, Mattie was finishing clearing away the coffee cups as Lola sat still softly stroking the wounded Malkin.

In answer to their questions about her sudden reappearance and distraught looks, Heather replied, "Betty and Tex. I think they're villains! Where's Brian? I need to tell him what happened." And she ran into the hall-way through the salon parlor toward the library.

In addition to the flames from the fireplace which threw dancing shadows on the rows of books, the light in the library came from a kerosene lamp on a table around which sat the three men in conference.

Don Diego Ramirez in his white shirt, still the dignified lord of the manor, looked worried. His eyes with the heavy brows were turned downward toward his big hands which drummed slowly on the tabletop.

Opposite him was Brian still wearing his denim jacket and rubbing his eyes slowly, his eyeglasses held in his other hand, as if he had been studying too many books for too long, searching for an answer to an unsolvable problem.

At the end of the table sat Pierre, his nervous energy seemingly evaporated, leaving him with an air of weariness. His black beret lay on the table before him, between his elbows, his hands slowly rubbing the top of his bald head. He had just repeated his decision to suggest a changed ending for the film, to call Rebel's Return a finished project, and leave the Castle as soon as possible.

Don Diego objected to the early departure. He was planning a special dinner for the principals of the cast and had hired the Sunshine Mariachi Band to play for the wrap party. "The New Mexico Power Company will arrive tomorrow, I am sure, and repair the transformer. It is inconvenient, I know, Señores, to go another time without showers and lights, but it is unnecessary to move to the Lazy-A ranch. A move at this time would be very difficult for you."

At that moment Heather entered the room and hearing Don Diego's final words, added a breathless agreement. "That's just what those people want. Don't go there." And she related her recent discoveries and the encounter with Tex. She was visibly shaken. Her pale face and frightened voice expressed her alarm.

Don Diego rose, startled into immediate anger. "I will call the police immediately. Those malvados cannot get away with this!"

Pierre straightened up and put on his beret as if returning to work. "No, no, Monsieur. There is no way to prove that they are the saboteurs. We must carry on as if we do not know what caused the generator to fail. And we will continue our work when the power comes back, but we will now be vigilant."

Brian's first reaction was concern for Heather. "Are you all right?" He put a gentle arm around her and led her to a chair. "A glass of water?"

Don Diego rang for refreshments, but Mattie had anticipated his request and was already coming through the doorway with a pot of coffee. Lola was behind her, bearing a tray of cups and cookies.

In retelling the story to the two women, Heather became more calm and the conference took on a determined vivacity as suggestions were exchanged. It was decided to proceed as usual with the special dinner, even inviting Betty and Tex. Because of his role as guard and watchman, Sam Redfox would be seated by Heather and during the party following would keep her in his sight. Heather would make no further allusions to the sugar sack nor convey any hint that she had expressed her suspicions to the others.

Don Diego seemed relieved that he could yet demonstrate his hospitality and prove the Adobe Castle the best hotel in the Southwest. Pierre looked resigned to postponing the final scenes of the filming. But Brian showed his continuing concern for Heather. "Are you sure you'll be O.K.? Shouldn't you have Lola or someone stay with you in the tower tonight?"

Lola put her coffee cup down and looked at Heather and Brian. "May I ask both of you to come with me for a separate little conference? Perhaps Mattie will care for Malkin in the kitchen while we talk in the Tower room."

Don Diego frowned momentarily, but in sympathy for Heather refrained from making any comments about the safety of the special suite.

Lola carried the lamp and led the way with Chippercat bounding ahead, chasing the shadow that leaped before him. Brian took Heather's hand in his, and it felt warm and reassuring as they followed the lamplight up the dark stairway.

Chapter XXI

Rest, rest, perturbed spirit!

—WILLIAM SHAKESPEARE

At the top of the stairway Lola paused and turned to Brian. "I had promised to investigate the Tower for Heather, and now that most of the crew are away, the Castle is more quiet. But I need to know about your willingness to help."

"I heard about Mickey's little tricks. Don't worry about me. I'll be quiet and try to keep an open mind."

As they entered the suite, a rush of cold air enveloped them and Heather went over to close the window. But it was already shut. Even though they had expected cool rooms due to the change in weather and the power outage, the breeze was baffling.

Lola asked them to sit at the card table and wait while she walked around the large room. Her hand holding the lamp trembled and she was visibly disturbed. "There has been a tragedy here," she said. "I feel great sadness and a sense of loss."

She returned to the table and placing the lamp on it, sank into the big chair near the table, leaned back, and closed her eyes.

Chippercat circled the room, this time ignoring the wastebasket, passing by the fringe on the draperies, and sniffing only once at the armoire. He jumped up onto the bed and curled up as if settled for the night. None of the subsequent activity in the room seemed to affect him.

Lola gave a long sigh and her head tilted back, one strand of reddish hair falling unheeded over her cheek. Her hands lay palm up in her lap, looking white and trembling against her long green flowered skirt. The moon pendant rose and fell on her breast and reflected the lamplight.

When she next spoke, her voice sounded strange, harsh and raspy, yet with a hollow timbre as if from inside a tunnel.

"Why do you come here? Who are you?"

Heather and Brian looked into the darkness to see whom she was addressing. Was Lola hearing an answer to her questions?

"Martin? Martin? Is that your surname or

given name?" Her breathing seemed more labored as she continued her questions.

"Why do you stay here? Do you know what year this is?"

After a pause she continued. "Over one hundred years have gone by since you died. You are free to pass to the other side now."

Lola's eyes closed, but tears began to roll down her cheeks. "Ann isn't here any more. You are free to leave." And after another pause she continued, "What shall we say? Not missing? Not missing? Major Chiv— Major Chiverton?"

A long pause ensued. Lola's eyelids quivered as if she were seeing a dramatic scene in a dream. Then she began sobbing. She shook her head as if witnessing a terrible scene. "Oh, no, no, no!"

Heather was frightened and whispered, "Is she in a trance? Shall we wake her? I'm scared."

Brian was staring at Lola as if in a trance of his own. Thoroughly mystified at the strange spellbound woman, he took Heather's hand and whispered, "I don't know. I don't know."

A sudden pounding at the door caused them to jump. The pounding proved to be from the physical world beyond the the door, and the voice following it was Mattie's. "Lola, can you come back down? This cat's going crazy and I don't know what to do!"

Lola's head turned toward the door and her eyes opened, but with a glassy and dazed look. Heather went to the door.

"All right, I'm coming. My head aches terribly. Give me a minute or two. I feel rotten. Come with me. Did you see him?"

"See who?" asked Brian.

"The soldier, a Union soldier from the Civil War. He was killed in this room. Oh, my God, it was horrible! Shot in the chest."

Heather knelt trembling at Lola's chair. "Who shot him?"

"Someone named Frank. Martin wanted to say goodbye to his sweetheart. He was to report to Major Chivver, or somebody Chiverton? He wanted to go back."

Mattie stared at the distraught Lola. Was she recounting a sad story from her own ancestry, or had she been concocting a tale to entertain the young couple and take Heather's mind off her earlier encounter?

Lola wiped her eyes and rising unsteadily said, "I'm coming. Poor Malkin could feel my distress. That's why she's uneasy. I'm O.K. now. I need an aspirin. My head is throbbing."

In the kitchen with the now calm Malkin on her lap, Lola retold her vision. "Heather, his sweetheart looked like you—the long dark hair.

The soldier thinks you are his sweetheart. He called her Ann. He was trying to say goodbye. The murder was terrible."

"Do you believe it's the actual ghost of a Civil War soldier?" Brian was astounded.

"Sometimes a person who dies under traumatic circumstances leaves a part of himself trapped here on earth with unfinished business. I tried to tell him he could go on to the other side, but I don't think I succeeded in convincing him."

Brian asked for more details. "Was there a Civil War battle fought near here? New Mexico wasn't even a state at that time. I didn't think the war came this far west."

Lola shook her head. "All I know is that it was one of the most vivid scenes I've ever experienced. Heather, you don't want to sleep there again tonight. There's an extra bed in my room."

Heather was about to agree when noise and laughter came from the courtyard. The guests, returning from the bear-watching expedition, entered the kitchen. The Tower séance was relegated to the shadows in favor of comments from the returning hayride.

Chapter XXII

There was a sound of revelry by night.

—George Gordon, Lord Byron

The returning guests were in merry spirits, and their comments were various.

"It was terrible. Couldn't see a thing. Big old flashlight trying to light up something clear across a canyon."

"But you could make out the bears. It was a mother and two cubs. I thought it was exciting."

"I didn't like Tex trying to shoot the mother bear. That was cruel."

"But it is hunting season in this area. The cubs are old enough to take care of themselves Tex said."

"Why would anyone want to kill a bear anyway? I'm glad he missed. I'm against guns and hunting."

"He'll eventually shoot one. He'll have a nice bear rug for the living room of the Lazy-A ranch house."

The latter comment was made by Jack Hilton. On another subject he added, "There's something funny going on with that couple. Betty was yammering on in an undertone to Tex, chopping him down for something or other. I couldn't make out what it was about, but they sure don't see eye to eye on something that went on today here at the Castle."

Heather and Brian looked knowingly at each other, and the short silence was broken by someone turning on the boom box radio and saying, "Let's party!"

Linda and Robbie started dancing to the music which was mostly a thumping bass echo accompanied by a woman's voice repeating, "Hug me, hug me, oh-oh-oh."

Mickey, standing near Brian and Heather, noticed that Lola was looking intently at Don Diego. "Look at her. I think she wants to dance with Don Diego. She's a psychic witch, and I'll bet she's putting a spell on him."

His comments proved prophetic. Don Diego stepped over to the radio and changed the frequency to a station that was playing golden oldies. He bowed in a courtly manner before Lola, swept her into the center of the kitchen, and guided her in great graceful circles to the music of "The Waltz You Saved For Me." They dipped and turned as if they had danced together for years. The younger couples ceased dancing and stood back in a ring to watch them. Don Diego, masterful and erect, was light on his feet, yet Lola responded to his touch instinctively, following the increasing complexity of his movements. And she seemed transformed. Her face glowed, the long green skirt swung in great circles as they turned, and she appeared young and happy. Heather was glad to see that the enchantment of the dance was erasing the horrible scene Lola had witnessed in her vision in the Tower.

Applause followed the end of the number and the audience asked for a repeat performance, but Don Diego surprised all of them again by commanding everyone to stand and dance.

"I will teach you. No one is permitted to sit. You do not need a partner. Just walk around the room and follow me."

It was a line dance with a walking pattern forward and back, repeated in the four directions. Soon everyone was laughing and clapping as they circulated around the big kitchen. Brian was pleased that the steps were simple enough for him to follow and that his ankle was strong enough to bear his weight smoothly. But he would have preferred a lesson in the traditional waltz that Don Diego had first performed with Lola. He wanted to hold Heather in his arms. She smiled at him, and as she faced away from him at each turn, he admired her slim figure and graceful movements.

"Look, Mattie is dancing too. And whoever thought Sam Redfox would join in!" Heather nodded at Brian for him to look in Sam's direction. Sam readily picked up the steps of the line dance because they were not unlike some of his traditional Pueblo dances, but his face remained an inscrutable mask of stoicism.

Linda and Robbie moved in a world of their own. Leaving in the beginning of the line dancing, they disappeared down the hallway and were not seen the rest of the evening.

At a pause in the music, Mickey raised his arms and asked for their attention. "This is the right time to distribute my carton of Cracker Jacks. Enjoy a snack break and get a fabulous prize at the same time!"

"Oh look, a mustache. Now I will be dashing and debonair."

"Siren whistle—just what I've always wanted."

"A tatoo. I know where I'll apply it!"

"I was wishing for a balloon and I got one."

Heather's prize was a miniature kazoo which she began humming into. She turned to Brian and asked to see his prize, but he tucked it into the pocket of his shirt and said, "Later, maybe. I need to fix it. It looks broken."

Heather was about to repeat her request to know what it was, when she found Lola beside her asking if she could talk to her in the hallway. She began with an apology. "I'm sorry if I frightened you with my reaction to the vision. I want you to know that the spirit of that young man cannot harm you. You are safe in the Tower. I don't know if he will return, but maybe you can send out thought waves telling him that you're not Ann. If you saw nothing tonight during my conversation with him, you will not witness any vision and certainly not the horrible scene I saw."

"I've slept in the Tower since I arrived," Heather replied, "and I think I'm brave enough to stay for two more nights. Now that I know a little about the ghost, I feel better. I feel sorry for him more than I feel afraid."

When the party ended and all the guests had gone to their rooms, Heather climbed the stairs with less reluctance than she had since her vacation began.

The Tower was quiet and no chill currents of air circulated. But to be on the safe side, before she blew out her candle, she sat upright in bed and shouted into the darkness, "I'm not Ann!"

Chapter XXIII

This then thou perceivest,
which makes thy love more strong,
To love that well which thou must
leave ere long.

—WILLIAM SHAKESPEARE

It is not to be determined whether the peace in the Tower room that night was due to Heather's exhaustion, her shouted warning into the darkness, or to the success of Lola's earlier adjurations to the tragic spirit. But it remains that Heather slept without disturbance until just before dawn when she was awakened by a soft scratching at the door. It was Chippercat, finished with his nightly prowls and longing for his favorite place on the downy soft coverlet of

Heather's bed. Heather opened the door to admit him, and before returning to bed, looked out the window at the line of light which presaged the coming of dawn along the Sangre de Cristo mountain range. In the darker sky above it hung the brilliant gem of the morning star and above that the slim moon, reduced to a thin letter C. She recalled the lopsided full moon of her arrival at the castle and wondered at how quickly the vacation days had passed. The moon had traveled backward among the stars, rising later and later each day, until now it could be seen only in the dawn hours. She wondered idly if it would bump into the morning star tomorrow, as it continued its eastward drop. Or perhaps Venus was moving too, and would be out of the way?

Her thoughts returned to Brian. Had the Tower séance convinced him of the reality of her experiences here? There could be no doubt that Lola's reactions were genuine, that there had been a supernatural presence in the room, but in the sober light of day, would Brian's scientific objectivity proclaim it was all a delusion? Why was his concurrence with her attitude so important to her? She realized that her regret at the ending of her vacation was due in great part to her admiration of the kindly blue eyes, gentlemanly demeanor, and air of strength about this handsome man. She had enjoyed the warmth of his hand, his concern for her after the threat from Tex, and the way he had looked at her during the dancing.

Where would Pierre be without Brian? She realized that Brian had to be more than just a site coordinator for the film company. His work showed that he had more than a small interest in the success of Rebel's Return. Perhaps he had backed the production with larger sums than were evident?

She returned to bed to sleep a little longer in the warmth of the big bed, and her dreams were of Brian. His firm jaw and chiseled features with the little round glasses gave him the look of Clark Kent, and she saw him removing his denim jacket and flying to the Lazy-A Ranch as Superman to sock Tex Belson with a blow that sent him flying to the ceiling against a comic book POW whose letters she could see hanging in the air even after Tex had fallen senseless to the floor. Then he gathered her in his arms to fly her to safety, his beard brushing against her face. Beard? Superman doesn't have a beard. She woke to find Chipper cuddled next to her face, his fur distorting the hero's appearance in her dream.

"I'm not Ann, and I'm not Lois Lane, either," she reminded herself. Time to face reality, think about packing, and get a few paragraphs written on her story. Perhaps she could write more on the train tomorrow. She certainly had material to write about and was grateful for the desire to commit it to paper.

Actors and extras were leaving the big kitchen as Heather returned from her run. She had jogged slowly, savoring the beauty of the forest the more because she was to leave it soon, and she wondered if any of the movie people felt a similar attachment to the big Castle and its beautiful setting. She had carried a camera in her waist pack and stopped to photograph her favorite views. Coming in by the patio, she stopped to stretch at the bench near the kitchen door.

The topic of conversation in the kitchen was the disappearance of Linda London. Pierre wanted to redo the final scene, but Linda was nowhere to be found. The red sports car and its owner were also missing, so the speculation was that the two lovers had driven away into the night. Their disappearance was not too surprising to Heather, but she had counted on Robbie to take her back to the train tomorrow. She would have to make an alternate plan in the event he did not return.

Mattie insisted on Heather's having the huevos rancheros, and although she didn't need the quantity of beans and the extra egg, Heather admitted that a little of the green chile added a piquancy that she was beginning to enjoy. If she could stay more than two weeks in the Southwest, perhaps she could really learn to appreciate the New Mexico cuisine.

Mattie was stewing in more than a culinary way this morning. "Look at this menu Don Diego wanted for tonight! There is no way I can prepare this stuff. In the first place I don't know what some of it is, and with the power off and no time to order catering from Santa Fe, he has got to be dreaming."

Heather looked at the menu. It would be a time consuming job for the most gourmet of chefs. And did Don Diego's cellars really have all these wines? There was listed Champagne to start: Gruet, Blanc de Noirs, an appetizer wine from Cakebread Cellars called Sauvignon Blanc, then Cabernet Sauvignon as the entree wine, and Johannisburg Reisling with the dessert.

"I can do the smoked lamb loin with papaya salsa that he wants for the entree," Mattie continued, "but Andalusian shrimp gazpacho with crustades for the soup, plus roasted piñon nut goat cheese empanadas topped with sautéed apples, as an appetizer? He's got to be kidding!"

"There's even a lime sorbet listed between

appetizer and entree," Heather noted. "Do you have that in the freezer?"

"Yes, but unless the power is restored darn quick, we'll have nothing but liquid lime mush. While the generator was going the freezer was O.K., and it'll hold for a few more hours, but I can't open it until the power comes back on."

"What is this Flan Cafe for dessert?" Heather asked.

Before Mattie could answer, Don Diego himself and Brian entered from opposite doors, both on urgent errands. Mattie turned to Don Diego, ready to request a reduced menu or a chef from Santa Fe, when suddenly the lights in the kitchen came on and a "Hooray" from the courtyard indicated that all power had been restored at the Castle.

The relief felt by everyone and the consequent adjustment in planning settled into a coffee-break conference at the big kitchen table. Heather rose to leave, but Don Diego asked her to remain. "Your opinion is important to us."

Don Diego seemed uncomfortable that the subject led to financial matters.

Brian was preparing to truck the failed generator back to Santa Fe and was estimating the cost of repairing the damage.

Mattie was deploring the projected expense of the elegant dinner with the catering or employment of an assistant chef. She reminded him that unless help from an unseen quarter were forthcoming, the Castle must close. The demands of the creditors were becoming insistent, Don Diego had been unable to retrench, and bankruptcy proceedings were the only alternative.

"Why don't we form a corporation?" As soon as the words were uttered, Heather stopped in shock. Had she really said that? What presumption on her part! To make any kind of suggestion in a matter which did not concern her was bad enough, but she had used the word "we" as if she were one of the concerned principals in the discussion.

A protracted silence ensued and Don Diego added, "I certainly will not sell. This is my ancestral property. My great grandfather was designated Hidalgo with special privileges from the crown of Spain. If I could continue with majority ownership, I would be willing to form a corporation to enable the Castle to continue as a great hotel."

Mattie reminded them of another obstacle. "The title has never been cleared, you know. Sam and his people from Santa Inés will claim their rights as prior owners. They'll argue that this is land belonging to the Pueblo Indian reservation. We'll have a legal tangle that will never end."

Brian saw a way around her objection. "Why not make Sam and his people partners also? Even if they will not invest a large sum, they may be satisfied to be listed as part owners and eventually share in some of the profits. And," he continued, "Pierre and I may be interested in buying some stock also. This place has great potential for future film making, and it would be in our interest to see the establishment continue."

Heather was emboldened by his words to add a further endorsement. "This would be a great place for conferences and educational symposia. Universities in the Midwest would love to have study sessions or summer school in a place like this."

Brian was trying to conceal his enthusiasm for the plan as he added, "I can see the film company's legal advisor today to get an idea of what our obligations would be and find out just what incorporation involves. I know you are concerned right now with the plans for the dinner and wrap party."

Mattie was pleased to see a way out of the dilemma. "Count me in," she said. "I can invest something in order to keep my job."

Lola LaFey entered the kitchen at that point, carrying Malkin. "I sense a happy atmosphere here," she said. "There is more positive energy in this kitchen than only that due to the restored electric power. I'm on my way to our final makeup session and predict a happy day for everyone."

Mattie and Don Diego adjourned to the library to go over the menu and meal problems. Brian was leaving for Santa Fe, but seemed reluctant to go. It seemed as if he was trying to say something to Heather and did not know how to begin. Heather tried to open the conversation. "When will you be back from Santa Fe?"

"I may miss the dinner, but I'll be back in time for the wrap party. You'll be here?"

"Oh sure. I don't leave until the afternoon train tomorrow. I may need a ride to Lamy station if Robbie doesn't show up."

"Even if he does, let me drive you down. We can stop for lunch in Santa Fe." He seemed relieved to have found a way to defer their conversation to a more private time and rose to leave.

Heather gave a cheery "See you later" and went out to retrieve her camera pack from the patio bench where she had left it, but stopped as she was halfway across the garden. "A bear!" she screamed. The furry black animal had climbed the old apple tree that hung over the patio wall and had dropped down on the inside when a branch gave way under his weight. Now he was sniffing at the garbage can and as Heather screamed, he knocked it over with a swipe of his paw.

Hearing her scream, Brian ran back through the kitchen and out the patio door. The bear was as alarmed as they were and began running toward the only open door, the patio door from which Brian had just emerged.

Next ensued a wild chase as Brian followed the bear around the kitchen, saying, "Shoo! Get out of here!" and Heather fumbled at the patio gate trying to unlatch it and escape to the courtyard. In her nervous haste she could not undo the latch, and as the bear reemerged from the kitchen, Brian called, "Heather! This way!" and he guided her along the wall back to the kitchen. When they were both inside, he slammed the door, trapping the bear in the patio. He put his arms around her and breathing heavily, they laughed with relief. Looking through the window nearest the door they saw the bear nosing at the camera pack. As it fell from the bench, the strap looped over the bear's head and the young bruin began an entertaining dance as he tried to disentangle himself from the belt and case.

Then Brian had an idea. "I'll try to open the patio gate from the outside. You bang on the door in here to scare him out." He ran out the side courtyard door of the kitchen to put his plan into effect, while Heather watched the bear go through more gyrations, finally freeing himself by breaking a strap. As the patio gate opened, he was more than willing to ignore the garbage and the apple tree and to make his escape by loping across the courtyard and into the canyon. Brian picked up the camera pack and returned through the patio to give it to Heather. She hugged him in gratitude and Brian prolonged the quick hug into an affectionate embrace which was promising to grow warmer. She felt his strong arms around her and his warm breath on her lips, but at that moment the film people came running in to determine the cause of the commotion.

Brian and Heather were retelling the scene with breathless laughter when Don Diego entered and restored their realization of the gravity of the situation. "You may say it is only an osito, a small young bear, but the mother is probably waiting just across the canyon. If she had been closer, you could have been in great danger. Do not go into the forest again."

Because she was leaving tomorrow, Heather realized she had had her last run at the Adobe Castle. She hoped the camera was still intact and regretted that she hadn't retrieved it in time to photograph the furry marauder.

The movie people resumed their activities, and Heather decided to organize her packing and prepare for the party. But at the top of the stairs, she was chagrined to discover she had forgotten to lock the door to the Tower room, and as she entered she realized someone had been there. In a vase made from a discarded milk carton was a bouquet of cardboard flowers—black roses!

At first she thought it was only a prank, but she became more alarmed remembering the encounter with Tex and recalling that black roses symbolized a death threat. She grabbed the crude vase and ran downstairs.

Don Diego was furious. Mattie tried to soft-pedal the incident and began suggesting they inform Mickey to determine if it was one of his tricks, but Sam reminded them of their planned stance of silence regarding any suspicions. The dinner preparations were in progress, the Bergens were there for the final scenes of the filming, and they would be at the table with the others for dinner. It would be reassuring to have Sam by her side for the evening, but oh, how she wished Brian had not left!

Chapter XXIV

Whoe'er excels in what we prize
Appears a hero in our eyes.

—Jonathan Swift

The dinner was a great success. With a combination of slight adjustment to the menu and the delivery of certain dishes from the La Fonda Hotel in Santa Fe, Don Diego was satisfied that he was offering his guests the finest cuisine in the state. The girls from the pueblo had not only baked the bread in the outdoor ovens, but also served the meal because Don Diego insisted that as an investor Mattie should be one of the honored diners. She had rehearsed the girls so that the courses would be presented properly. Attired in a long blue dress with her hair pinned back, she looked like a chic chatelaine as she nodded her signals to the Indian girls, pleased with their service. The candlelight shone on the burnished silver and the crystal glasses, Malkin sat in a basket by the china cabinet, and Chippercat took his usual post atop the cabinet, matching the high position to his superior air.

The dessert Flan turned out to be a delicious pudding, covered with piñon nuts, served in a chocolate chalupa shell on a plate drizzled with chocolate and rimmed with dollops of whipped cream and sweet cherries. Each person declared himself to be too full to dance, but as the mariachis warmed up their instruments and the trumpet notes rose, the assembled party took to the dance floor in the big kitchen and repeated the line dances they had learned. They leaped around in polkas and two-steps as the rhythms changed.

Heather looked in vain for Brian. Her first partner, as promised, was Mickey, and his lively banter brought smiles to her face, helping conceal her disappointment over the missing partner. Betty and Tex were stomping the lively tunes, Tex's long legs and thin torso a contrast to Betty's portly bulk. Don Diego and Lola repeated their graceful demonstration, and then Don Diego surprised the entire company by initiating a new practice, designed to vary the activity, by cutting in and forcing everyone to trade partners. He began by tapping Mickey on the shoulder and sweeping Heather away from him. Mickey grabbed Lola, and other couples began exchanging partners.

Suddenly Heather found herself dancing with Tex. Taking advantage of the wild cadence of the two-step, he swung her faster and faster, squeezing her hand in a painful grip and pulling her body close to his. She tried to say "Stop!" but it was only a breathless objection unnoticed by everyone else. He was deliberately trying to hurt her and his words confirmed his menacing purpose. "Do you like black roses? Your next bouquet will be lilies—white ones." Only the pause in the music at the end of the number caused him to release her. She looked for Sam, but Jack Hilton took her hand and began to dance the now slower number. He had noted her distress and asked her to explain.

After the end of the number, he stepped to the musicians and asked them to pause for a short interlude. "Ladies and Gentlemen, it's time for a special entertainment. For you old hands, this is nothing new, but some of you have asked how the fake fights are staged for the movies. If I can call Tex Bergen up here, to pretend to fight with me, I'll demonstrate how the movies make a little pushing around look like a serious bashing."

There was a puzzled hush, and after Jack repeated the invitation, Tex sauntered forward. Jack explained, "Now we'll pretend that you've insulted a certain young lady, and I've called you a rotten skunk. You're going to swing at me, but I'll duck. Then I'll swing at you and these good people watching will slam one fist into the other palm as I pretend to hit you."

Tex looked apprehensive but curled his fists and straightened up to wait for the signal. At Jack's "Now!" he swung, and Jack ducked. But before he finished the swing Jack returned it with a hard blow, connecting with Tex's chin and sending him reeling back to the wall. The requested sound effects were too late but they echoed the real crack everyone heard as fist connected with jaw. Tex looked dazed and staggered to remain upright.

"Oops! You were supposed to duck. Sorry about that." Jack's polite apology was delivered in a sarcastic tone. "Let's try the next trick. I'll grab you by the shirt front, and slam you into a chair that will collapse." And he matched the action to the words. But the chair did not collapse, and Tex received a bone-jarring crash as his tall frame collided with the unyielding chair.

By this time everyone realized that Jack was settling a real score under the guise of a demonstration. They stood spellbound watching the short older man make a fool of the tall young cowboy, and everyone expected Don Diego to end the fracas. Betty called out "Stop!" and Jack picked up her words as his cue.

"Now your wife will run forward and try to stop the fight, but we're all alone in this shack, you see, and it does no good. I'll pretend to give you one more blow and end with the traditional bum's rush. First, I'll say those good ol' words: you get outta here and never darken this door again, and if I catch you round my gal, or round my cattle or near my generator, I'll have you strung up on the nearest tree. Now git!"

As Tex ducked, Jack came at him with an uppercut that sent him sprawling, then turned him over and lifting him bodily by his belt, dragged him toward the door. Sam was at the door and had it open by the time Jack was there to throw the hapless cowboy outside. Betty followed him crying and threatening to call the law.

The circle of spectators clapped and Jack bowed. Then he added, "We'll also pretend that my hand is mighty sore from hitting that skunk and someone can pretend to bring me some ice so I can wrap it up and cool it down."

Presaged by only a few distant rumbles of

thunder, the rain that night came down steadily and hard. Instead of a monsoon shower, it was an all night "soaker." The steady thrumming of the falling drops after the excitement of the wrap party was conducive to deep sleep for everyone, including Heather. Snug in her Tower, she slept so soundly she did not even dream of the missing Brian.

She finally wakened to the insistent mewing of Chipper at the door wanting out. When she opened the door, there stood Malkin, as if waiting for Chipper, having come to pick him up for a dawn ramble. Heather smiled to see them go down the stairs together. Before she returned to bed, she looked out the window. Only a hint of the coming day outlined the mountain range, and there was the very thin moon hanging just over it. But where was Venus?

As she stared, wondering sleepily, it suddenly appeared. The moon really had passed in front of it and now the morning star, emerging from the dark top of the darkened disc looked for all the world like a huge diamond glittering against the dark sky. The waning crescent of the moon became the thin silver ring that supported it. The diamond ring in the sky! She remembered Lola's prediction, and even as she gloried in the beauty of the sight, she regretted that, though probably rare, she was seeing an actual and natural event, not the personal vision she had expected. Lola had said the diamond ring would be important, and given the rarity of being treated to this celestial sight, she believed it so, but she had connected it in her mind with Brian and the possibility of the deepening feelings they shared.

And where was Brian? She hoped he had returned in the night and had not been stranded in the rain with a broken down vehicle. She returned to bed with a sigh, hoping for a little more sleep before she finished packing to leave the Castle.

Daylight brought dazzling sunlight with a perfectly clear sky, but the air was crisp with the promise of an early autumn. Heather sat on her suitcase close to the adobe wall where the sunshine seemed to magnify the heat, holding her yellow pad of lined paper ready to record parting thoughts about the Castle.

She had said goodbye to Mattie in the kitchen and complimented her on her appearance at the previous evening's dinner. Heather believed that Mattie's inclusion as a partner in the Castle's corporation had given Mattie new pride in her appearance and an inclination to cooperate with Don Diego instead of contradicting him.

Jack Hilton emerged from the gateway carrying his suitcase. Heather rose to thank him for his part in defeating the villains from the Lazy-A. She asked for his autograph on her yellow pad and as he signed it with a swollen hand, she realized that her movie hero had become her real live hero indeed.

Next Lola came out carrying the cat cage in which Malkin paced restlessly. She was followed by Don Diego with Chippercat at his heels. Don Diego didn't realize that Lola had conjured up a spirit in the Tower room. What would he say, Heather wondered, if he were told? He seemed attracted to this charming sorceress, perhaps enough to accept her liaison with the spirit world which he had ridiculed?

Lola set the cage down while she and Don Diego spoke together in low and confidential tones. Chippercat sniffed at the cage, then put a paw on the screened doorway as if trying to talk to Malkin. Malkin's paw emerged, touching Chippor's as if shaking hands goodbye. Lola and Don Diego noticed the gesture, laughed, then continued talking. As they shook hands, Heather saw him slip something to Lola which looked like a tiny silver box. Lola smiled her thanks and put it into her purse. Heather looked away, not wanting to intrude in what was becoming a very tender farewell.

At breakfast Lola had smiled knowingly at Heather's description of the diamond ring in the sky. Now she put a little card into Heather's hand and said, "Here's my address. You must let me know if the rest of my prediction comes true." Then she climbed into the green-room van and was gone.

The morning melted away as did the film people, their vans and big trucks pulling out of the courtyard every few minutes, till the Castle sat quiet in the mountain sunshine. But where was Brian? She kept looking at her watch and estimating the time required for the drive to Lamy. Even if he arrived now, it was too late for lunch at Santa Fe. They would barely make it to the station on time.

One of the last guests to depart was Mickey. Afterwards, she believed that he had been waiting till the others had left before approaching her. "Still waiting for Brian? I think you'd better give up on him. The Santa Fe girls probably made things too interesting for him to leave."

Affecting nonchalance, she laughed, "Maybe so, but there's still time. If he doesn't make it, I'm sure Don Diego will find me a ride to Lamy station."

"Why not let me take you? I'm all ready, and there's a cozy seat next to me in my little truck."

She began to demur when he continued, "I'd like to take you all the way to California. You already have your actor's license. Let me put you in pictures. I know the man to see for your screen test."

She began to object more strongly, but still not believing he was serious.

Then he pulled her into a standing position and embracing her recited, "Come live with me and be my love. And we will all the pleasures prove."

Laughing, she pushed him away but realized even if Brian did not appear, she would never accept a ride with Mickey. She couldn't trust him to take her only as far as Lamy.

The dilemma was solved as Don Diego came forward. He had witnessed Mickey's ardor and explained as he approached, "The Adobe Castle furnishes transportation to the station. Our insurance will not allow any other company to transport our guests. Sam Redfox is our official driver and is ready to go when you wish."

"I'll follow you then," said Mickey. "I can see you off at the train anyway."

Sam, who had been waiting nearby, finally walked over and picked up Heather's bag, motioning for her to get into his pickup. But just as she was about to get in, they heard a car approaching.

The happy anticipation on Heather's face faded to disappointment as the car drew up and, instead of the expected Brian, there emerged the curmudgeon and his daughter. He held out his hand introducing himself. "Hi! Remember me from the church hayride? Charles Kinney, and this is my daughter Elaine. We're leaving to go back to Iowa, but I'd like to see this castle before we go. Maybe book a reservation for next year. Did you ever get rid of the ghost? Hope your vacation was better than ours. That Lazy-A is a disaster, no hospitality or efficiency, owners arguing all the time, and the woman brought him home from a drunken brawl last night all beat up."

Sam shook his hand, gave his own name in response, and directed them to the front gate. He and Heather started down the mountain. Even with her heavy heart, she was not immune to the glory of the morning and the beauty of the forest. As they came into a clearing, she asked, "What are those big golden bushes?"

"Chamisa. *Chrysothamnus nauseosus.*" And that was the extent of his conversation the rest of the trip.

The road gave evidence of the severity of the previous night's storm, big gullies and eroded washouts slowing their progress. But Sam powered the big pickup skillfully around the holes and left Mickey so far behind that he probably was lost at the second turn in their route.

As they reached the main road Heather became aware of a furry object rubbing against her leg. It was Chippercat. He had jumped into the truck when they were greeting the Kinneys. She picked up the usually distant animal and was surprised that he did not resist, but for the first time allowed her to hold and pet him. She bent her head close over him and concealed a few tears in his fur.

The train was on time. Sam carried her bag to the platform and shook her hand. In response to her "Thanks for everything," he replied, "You'll be back."

"I hope so." She waved to the gray cat, who was watching through the windshield from the dashboard of the truck, and boarded the train. As the big Southwest Chief pulled out of the station, Heather looked out the window, her eyes searching the road for Brian, but she saw only Sam's pickup making its way up the hill back toward the Adobe Castle.

Chapter XXV

Everything will turn to account when love is once set going, even the sandwich tray.

—JANE AUSTEN

The members of Senior Scout Troop 614, en route to Philmont National Scout camp from Los Angeles, were assembled in the dining car of the Southwest Chief. Their natural liveliness was augmented by their recent release from the smog of the city and further enhanced by the prospect of several days in the mountains of New Mexico. Two of the more lively boys were entertaining the others by juggling the foil-wrapped butter pats that had been served with the crescent rolls as a prelude to the noon lunch.

Heather sat at a table occupied by two of the younger Scouts facing an elderly woman who wore a pained expression. The jugglers were being razzed by their audience with eager cries of "Drop it, drop it, drop, drop, drop!"

The pained lady's pinched expression was due to the rowdiness of the boys and her disapproval became obvious as the two at her table began giggling. She frowned with disapproval at their hilarity.

Several tables away, the Scout leader, a tall thin bespectacled man, was trying to ignore the boys and, by chatting with the middle aged couple at his table, tried to give the impression that he was not connected to the rowdy noisemakers. A tall heavy headwaiter was adding to his discomfiture with his hearty laughter and amused approval of their antics.

As the train began to slow in its approach to a station, the lady with the pained expression left the car to search for a more peaceful luncheon spot in the lounge car. The diners heard the announcement, "Next station stop is Lomas, Lomas, New Mexico," and Heather turned to peer out of the window.

Then she half rose from her chair and cried out, "Brian! It's Brian. I believe that man is looking for me!"

Brian had slammed the door of the van and was running toward the train. The red-haired Scout sitting next to Heather caught the urgency in her voice, and said, "I'll go get him and tell him you're here. What's your name? Heather? I'll bring him to the diner car." He left the table and ran through the next car toward the coaches where the Lomas passengers were boarding.

The stop at tiny Lomas was very brief, and the train was moving again before the red-haired boy returned with Brian following him.

"Heather! I'm sorry I didn't get back in time. The Rio bridge was washed out and I had to drive clear around by Española. I missed you at Lamy and drove like mad this seventy miles. I didn't think I'd make it." He paused to steady himself against the table as the swaying train picked up speed. His face was flushed with exertion and embarrassment as he realized he was becoming the focus of everyone's attention. "I was going to persuade you to stay. I want you to be a partner in our venture, that is, I'd like to ask if—"

As he paused in his explanation, the first butter-juggler boy caught the situation and began to chant, "Ask her. Ask her. Kiss, kiss, kiss!" The other boys picked up the refrain and soon everyone was smiling at the embarrassed couple.

The head waiter approached and asked, "Are

you here for lunch, Sir? Soup or salad?"

"No, I just got on. I mean yes, I'll take salad." He sat down in the empty seat opposite Heather. "Will you, would you, get off with me at the next stop and come back to the Castle?"

Before Heather could reply, they were interrupted by the conductor who had followed him and was asking for his ticket. It took several minutes to settle the confusion, and the conductor was completing the sale to Brian of a one-way ticket to Raton, the next stop two hours away, when the train entered a tunnel. The waiter who had returned with a tray of salads grasped the opportunity of reigniting the hilarity with an antic that he had previously determined to be a guaranteed entertainment: He brought the back of his own hand to his lips and made a big kissing sound in the darkness, followed by a smack as he clapped his hands together. As the train emerged from the tunnel and everyone was visible again, his voice boomed out, "Now who done got kissed? And who got slapped for it? He gave a knowing wink toward the embarrassed couple, and his deep rumbling laughter was echoed by the other passengers.

As the laughter died down, the jolly waiter began some friendly attempts at relieving their discomfiture, aided by the conductor who left saying, "Well, you have two hours to get it all fig-ured out. You may as well enjoy your meal."

Over Pasta a la Southwest, followed by caramel sundaes, Brian told of his visit to the Santa Fe legal firm and to the archives of the State Library and the New Mexico Museum, where research assistants had showed him not only the old land grant deeds to the Castle prop-erty, but also some Civil War documents corrobo-rating the names Lola had learned in her vision.

"It was Chivington, Major Chivington, the name Lola was trying to say. He was commander of the Union forces at the battle of La Glorieta Pass in 1862. It was the major battle of the war in the West. And they showed me the list of casual-ties. There was a Phillip Martin listed among the missing!"

"Not missing, not missing," Heather cried. "Do you remember when she said that?"

"The poor guy wanted someone to tell the Commander what had happened. His soldier days were cut off by a jealous rival in love, I guess. The whole thing made a believer of me, I tell you. I'm sorry I doubted your stories about the haunting in the Tower."

He reached over to take her hand and repeated his proposal. "Don't you think we'd make a good team helping to run the Adobe Castle?"

"Are you asking me to marry you?"

"Well, yes, I mean, I've decided you're my kind of gal. Could you see yourself in a partnership with a guy like me?"

"I am beginning to think you're my kind of guy," Heather admitted. "But I'm not ready to commit to a partnership until I feel that I can make my own way first. I want to finish my degree at college. I want to write. I want to prove myself. I want to write the winning story in the contest."

"You can still do that and be my wife."

"But not now. I have commitments at home. I'm enrolled for the fall term. I really want to put my ideas on paper, and I've decided my story will be a gothic romance instead of a murder mystery."

"Will it take place at an Adobe Castle in the Southwest?"

"Yes, and it will have ghosts and cats and movie cowboys."

"Will it have a prince who tried many times to be a hero to the princess and succeeded only in beating up her brother?"

"The prince in my story rescues the princess from a vicious bear."

"Will you write that the prince almost killed himself trying to get on the train and propose to the princess?" And he pulled out a little tin ring with a huge faux gem at the top and placed it on her finger. "It's adjustable because it's from the Cracker Jack box. One size fits all. But in your story you can say it's real."

"And in my story I'll write that the prince said the proper words. He said he loved the princess."

"Yes, write that. Write that he loved her very much, and that she loved him."

They looked at each other and laughed. They adjourned to the coach car and continued their tête-à-tête. Heather told of Jack's drubbing of the evil Tex, and Brian gave more details of the plan for the business incorporation of the Adobe Castle. And they spoke of the many other important issues that lovers must decide.

The Raton station stop came all too soon. Brian went to find the conductor and ask about transportation back to the Castle from Raton. When he returned to her seat, Heather accompanied him down the little stairway to the lower level of the car where passengers disembark, and between long and sweet embraces they continued their promises regarding phone calls, letters, Christmas visits, and reservations for a church reception hall.

The Scouts were leaving at Raton also, and seeing the ring on Heather's hand, the red haired boy offered his congratulations and shook Brian's hand.

Heather stood in the doorway until the waving Brian could no longer be seen, and as she turned to go back up the little stairway, the conductor informed her that the gentleman who had just left the train had purchased a private roomette for her for her overnight ride to Chicago. He would show her to the first-class car and bring her luggage there.

In her private bedroom Heather found a writing table that unfolded from beneath the window. She opened it, placed her yellow lined tablet on it and began writing, "The lucky young woman had won a two-week vacation at a place called the Adobe Castle."

Inez Ross is a freelance writer who does travel arti-cles for the Los Alamos *Monitor*. Her *Strange Dis-appearance of Uncle Dudley; A Child's Story of Los Alamos* is a local best seller. She lives in Los Alamos, New Mexico, where she is currently hik-ing on and writing about the Santa Fe Trail.